WINTER WRITERLAND

A DAISY MCFARLAND COZY MYSTERY

BEATRICE FISHBACK

(Paperback) ISBN: 9781973304470

ACKNOWLEDGMENTS

Thank you to so many great women in my life—on both sides of the pond…

Renie Onorato: For the continuous encouragement and support in designing beautiful covers, professional editing and formatting.

Linda Robinson and Dana K. Ray: For the years of being critique partners.

Priscilla Malkin: My dear English friend who is also a wonderful cultural insider and editor.

Huge thanks to Swanwick Writers' Summer School mates: Fiona Park, Jennifer Wilson, Allison Symes and Val Penny. Without their friendships, fabulous imaginations and willingness to be a part of this wee story, Winter Writerland would never have been born.

To Jim: Whatever writing I accomplish is because of your willingness to sacrifice the time it takes to fulfill my dreams. I can't imagine embarking on this endeavor without your love and support.

WINTER WRITERLAND

CHAPTER 1

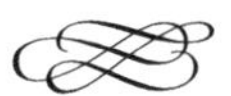

A long pair of scissors plunged into the unsuspecting victim's neck. The razor-sharp edge pierced skin, tissue, and muscle. An artery burst with balloon-type pressure and spattered black-red liquid...

Meow.

Daisy McFarland stopped typing. The adamant cry shattered her concentration into a zillion pieces, and the determined thousand words she had intended to write stopped mid-stream.

Her cat, Pillow, was fluffier than a massive bag of cotton balls, but not as soft and nowhere near as cuddly.

She shoved away from her desk, walked the three paces to a cupboard, filled a bowl with dry GoCat, placed it on the brown-tiled kitchen floor and stepped away. Pillow was not a force to be reckoned with.

The cat sauntered up, belly dragging, and began to eat with that haphazard way of hers. She tossed pieces of cat food in the air, aimed chunks into the nearby water bowl and intentionally created the biggest mess possible. She gazed up at Daisy with a disparaging smile to see if she made her mistress upset. Daisy adored the creature. Pillow was everything she wasn't. Bold and gregarious, the animal let anyone within earshot know she was queen of the castle. Whereas Daisy had been nicknamed mouse by her fellow teachers because of her squeaky voice and small stature, Pillow was strong and determined and would only be held by someone on her terms. Which meant kneading you to death and shredding whatever outfits were worn at the time before settling down. Daisy had plenty of tattered clothes to prove it.

"Now Pillow. You must behave yourself while I'm away. I'm sure Rosemary will be very good to you, but last time, you nearly clawed every inch of skin off her calf. You must be kinder to people."

The cat chewed another piece of dry food with a loud crack and looked at Daisy as if she had asked her to run in front of a Mac truck and not wince when she was hit.

Daisy patted the cat's head and proceeded upstairs. The two-bedroom, British Victorian terraced house on High Street in Worlingburgh was as soundproof as a music studio. She could throw shoes at the walls if she wanted and those on either side of her place would never be the wiser. Not that she would ever throw her shoes. She only had five pairs—one in each basic color.

A large stack of elementary school books covered the dresser. After thirty years of teaching in North Carolina, it was hard to part with them. Her time to retire had been set and she'd been happy to proceed, but she missed those children dreadfully.

A swipe of her hand and the layer of dust off the top of the books vanished into thin air. She threw the lot of them onto the bed and filled the now empty spot with an oversized burgundy suitcase.

A photo of her with four other teachers sat front and center on the bedside table. They had been cruel and kind at the same time and Daisy never quite knew where she stood when in their presence. But it had been her life, a safe routine that had morphed into a comfortable rut.

She flipped the suitcase open and began to pack. The annual writing week in Branick was the one way she spoiled herself each year. Daisy looked forward to being with other writers. The buzz.

Chatter about what characters would do in each person's attempt to create a masterpiece novel that would seemingly come alive during their time together.

Ding Dong.

Daisy tossed a gray, frayed sweater on top of the growing stack of clothes and proceeded down the narrow stairs to the front door.

Meow.

"Now, girl. I'm sure it's not for you. Please move away."

The cat sat front and center at the bottom of the stairs and made opening the door a formidable challenge.

Daisy lifted Pillow with both hands, cradled the middle of the cat's oversized, fur-balled stomach and puffed. "The vet was right. You do need to lose weight."

Meow. The cat pushed herself out of Daisy's clutch and waddled toward the sofa. She shoved herself under it with great effort like someone trying to fit a size-ten foot into a size-five shoe.

Daisy yanked the door open.

Rosemary Wood, large wool hat perched sideways on her head, carried a pair of pruning shears and stepped inside. The flowered gloves she wore came from the local National Trust. Everyone Rosemary's age wore them with great pride as if they were somehow partnered with the elaborate company that owned hundreds of estates across Great Britain. Her face was filled with friendly crinkled lines. Ever since the first day they met three years before in London when Daisy first arrived in country and she'd saved Daisy's life, Rosemary's grin had stayed in place.

"Why Rosemary, I wasn't expecting to see you until tomorrow. And what in the world are you doing gardening on a day like today? Come in. Come in before you catch cold."

"A gardener never stops even when the plants sleep. We must keep up with them summer or winter." She jabbed the shears in the air with a thrust. "You'd do well to come out and prune your rose bushes a bit."

"But it's freezing. Those plants need their cover to stay warm."

"Mulch works wonders."

"I'm sure it does, but I'd rather let them stay dressed just the way they are."

Rosemary chuckled as she took off her gloves, coat and hat, and slid off her wellies.

"Cup of tea?" Daisy's wispy breath escaped outside just before she closed the door.

"Lady Grey if possible. Please." A transplant to

Worlingburgh from London, Rosemary's accent was still strong.

"You know I always keep some on hand for you. Besides, I've come to like it myself." Daisy filled the kettle and placed a teabag in each of the cups. "Biscuit?" A plate of McVitie Dark Chocolate Digestives waited on the sideboard.

"No, thank you. I'm watching what I eat these days."

"That's no fun."

"Of course it isn't." Rosemary snatched a biscuit and laughed. "How's the novel coming?"

"I'm stuck on how to commit the perfect crime. But I'm sure I'll learn some tips at the conference." Daisy poured hot water into two mugs.

Rosemary shook her head. "Imagine a group of people meeting to design the ideal murder and no one being the wiser."

"It's all in great fun."

"I'm sure it is. But I cringe at the sight of blood, even a small cut. I can't imagine writing an entire story about death and dying." Daisy's neighbor shuddered. "Now tell me how our Pillow's doing." She nodded toward the cat whose hind legs were visible beneath the couch.

"She's as spunky as ever. Don't take any abuse from her. I've already warned her that she'd better behave while I'm away or she'll have to answer to me when I get home."

"Pillow answers to no one."

Daisy squeaked a rubber toy and Pillow's legs went from sight as she pulled herself further under. "So true."

"Of course, she'd have to answer to someone if she committed a murder like her mistress is trying to do."

Daisy giggled. "Touché."

Rosemary dipped the biscuit. "I stopped by to pick up your keys and reassure you that Pillow will be fine."

Daisy retrieved a set of spare house keys from a small hook behind the door. "I thought you were coming tomorrow."

"Turns out my mum has an appointment. I need to drive her to the surgery."

"Everything okay?"

"There's concern about a spot on her nose." Rosemary shrugged. "She's ninety. She's bound to have something. Other than the spot, she's quite healthy."

"You're sure you don't mind keeping an eye on things? What if your mum needs you?"

"It's not a problem, I assure you." Rosemary took the keys.

Pillow popped out from under the sofa with

Pillsbury doughboy finesse, stretched and ambled up the stairs.

They laughed in unison. "If you fail to feed her for the entire time I'm gone, she would still need to lose weight."

Rosemary finished her tea, headed to the front door and pulled on her wellies. "Enjoy your trip to Branick. How will you get to the train station?"

"Toni's Taxi."

"I'm sorry I can't take you."

"Not a problem. This is my third year and I've got the routine down to a science."

"Enjoy your holiday." Rosemary gathered her coat, gloves, and headed out.

Daisy went upstairs to finish what she'd started.

Pillow sat smack dab in the middle of the suitcase. The heavy sweater on top pulled to pieces as if the animal planned on nesting a brood right then and there.

Tsk. "Wish I had *you* down to a science. You are a natural phenomenon beyond explanation."

CHAPTER 2

Frost, in fragile lace-like doilies, decorated the lower half of the windowpane. Daisy perched on tiptoe and looked over the lacework. School would be delayed for certain. She set the thermostat up a degree and tied the sash of her soft-blue robe.

Maybe going to Branick was futile. Weather conditions this time of year were extremely unpredictable. She stomped a pink slippered foot in defiance. Nothing would keep her from this event.

BBC announced the forecast on her computer's app. "Temperatures are quite low this morning. Black ice on the M1 is causing delays."

She would have to get an earlier start, which meant Pillow would be alone longer than she had anticipated.

Daisy penciled her mobile number on a napkin for Rosemary and left it on the table, although she was certain she already had it.

After a quick shower, she dressed in layers. Leggings covered by beige corduroy trousers, Under Armor shirt with a green sweater, and the Icelandic outfit was complete.

Toni's Taxi honked. She tossed last minute toiletries into the suitcase, snapped it shut and dragged it down the stairs.

Pillow blocked her path.

"Now, now. You must let me go. I'll only be gone a week."

The cat sauntered away without a peep.

"The least you could do is say goodbye."

Meow.

"Thank you. I'll miss you, too." She blew a kiss, put on her coat, and exited the house.

To die. To die. To die. Daisy's brain registered *to die,* rather than the usual click-clack as the train started to move. She stared at her computer screen and urged her mind to formulate something, anything for her novel. Dreams of becoming a New York

Times Bestseller were far fetched, but she had to give it a try.

Although the train departed several hours after the scheduled time and others were quite upset at the delay, she had time to spare. Since retirement, Daisy had *plenty* of time. More than she cared for, in fact.

Besides Pillow and Rosemary, it had been difficult making friends in the small English village she called home. Children whizzed past the front of her house daily on their way to primary school further down the street. Their laughter rang with sweet familiarity. Daisy had tried to speak to the mothers as they strolled behind their offspring, but they were busily engaged in conversations with each other. She was a teacher has-been.

Clickity-clack, to die, clickity-clack, to die. The train picked up speed. Undulating hills sparkled with a thin layer of snow and trees glistened with frozen water droplets. A magical winter wonderland.

Daisy returned to the computer screen. The snow-white blank page was nowhere near as lovely as the outside scenery. In fact, it was downright depressing.

Another passenger walked past and stopped. Nearing a hundred if she had to guess, a thin elderly man who looked like a character from Dickens sat across from her. The good-sized table between the rows kept him at a safe distance.

The distinct odor of mothballs reeked like essence of antiquity from his tweed suit and the waistcoat that matched. Faded twinkles in his eyes gleamed as he smacked his toothless mouth and winked. Could he truly be flirting?

She hunkered further over the computer. At fifty-three she was aware her attractiveness had faded along with her bronze-colored hair. But surely there was someone she could meet who wasn't as old as Methuselah.

"What ya doin?" The man asked.

"Writing a book." Perhaps a curt reply would give him a clue she was busy and wasn't interested in his sleazy overtures.

"About what?" He leaned toward her on his elbows. Creaking and popping came from his mummified bones.

Guess he didn't get the clue. "The perfect *murder*."

His twinkles disappeared and the dog-wrinkles around his mouth drooped. The man picked up his cane and weaved slightly with the train's jerk as he stood and moved to another section while looking suspiciously over his shoulder at her.

Daisy smiled and winked. She might not be able to pen a complete sentence on the laptop, but words still had power when spoken with conviction.

Branick Station was about as big as an outhouse with one small waiting area, a loo, and a ticket machine. So why in the world did she have to walk an eternity, cross up and over the tracks and back down again to reach the small enclosure?

Fortunately, there was a young man with his small son in tow who left the train at the same time. He carried Daisy's suitcase the distance while the little boy chattered nonstop. "Da, who's that lady? Is she a stranger? You told me never to talk to someone I don't know. Do you know her?"

The father answered with patience befitting a lawyer to a jury, "She's a nice lady who needs our help."

With a shake of his shoulders, the little tot skipped next to his dad without a care in the world.

Father and son walked Daisy to the taxi that waited curbside.

"I'm so sorry I'm late. I tried to ring the taxi but there wasn't any connection on the train." Sweat dripped under Daisy's Under Armor in spite of the cold tunnel of air swirling the small entourage.

"Weren't your fault." The scruffy driver lifted her luggage into the boot and got behind the wheel. Daisy sat behind him, closed the door and waved goodbye to her two helpmates. The little one waved with enthusiasm as if they'd known each other forever.

"Branick Conference?" The driver looked at her through the rearview mirror.

"Yes, please."

Taxi drivers were notorious for either talking too much or not saying a word. In the silence of the cab, Daisy reviewed the contents of the brown envelope filled with information about the week, which included a map of Branick and a catalog of teachers and classes on offer. The sprawling Branick manor had once been someone's private residence during the 1850's and then used as a POW camp during WWII. Over the years it had been converted and now the U-shape had two short wings that served as rooms for various classes. A long glassed-in porch along the center section was where tea and coffee were served during morning and afternoon breaks—a must have in British culture. It was also where the dining room and library could be found.

When the driver arrived at the center, the low jabber of voices from Waterside Block—her home for the next seven days—was a welcomed reprieve from the silent treatment the taxi driver had imposed.

Strings of small, twinkling white lights hung over

each section of the manor like pearl necklaces. Wreaths and holly were tacked in various places, giving the appearance of the perfect Christmas card.

Waterside Block was one of three separate buildings that housed guests who attended various functions throughout the year.

Fiona Banks came running out of the building, arms wide open. She scooped Daisy into her arms and squeezed as if to pop her head off. "I'm so happy to see you. I've missed you."

Daisy hugged in return and released her friend. "I was so glad you were able to make it."

"I wouldn't miss it for the world. John had to travel on business and the girls have their own plans this week. But we'll be together as a family on Christmas Day."

"I'm so grateful the committee decided to offer a smaller venue right before Christmas. It's an ideal time for those of us who might be on our own."

Fiona grabbed her hand. "It'll be lovely being together, won't it?"

"I understand the staff will be smaller and there won't be as many attending."

"I know. Isn't that marvelous? We'll have undivided attention from those teaching the courses."

"So where are Jen and the others?"

"They're unpacking. Let's go inside, shall we?"

They headed in, clasping each other's hands. Cups of hot chocolate and plates of finger sandwiches awaited: cheese and tomato, cucumber, salmon and cream cheese. Crusts were cut off and curlicue red and green veggies sat alongside adding festive color.

Fiona pulled out a bottle of Prosecco from a Sainsbury's bag. "You're the last of our lot to arrive. Some new attendees will be coming later on, but right now, this time's for us."

Daisy's insides shimmered with expectations of long chats, a ton of creative energy and flowing rivers of wine. Forget being a New York Times bestseller, friendships in life and a week at Branick were what mattered most.

CHAPTER 3

Laughter from outside Daisy's bedroom wafted under the door. She rolled over and waited for the next round of sound. The warm duvet wrapped like a cocoon and her temples throbbed from last night's Prosecco. It would take a lot to motivate her to crawl out from under the feathers.

Giggle. Giggle. Snicker. Snicker.

Daisy unwrapped herself, shuffled to the door and opened it slightly. A laser beam of hallway light pulsed her eyes and she squinted.

Jen, Fiona, Allison and Val stood in a half-circle like the pillared rocks of Stonehenge. Then burst out in laughter.

"You have your nightie on backwards." Fiona pointed and smiled.

"What were you up to last night that we don't know about?" Jen's brows rose and the twinkle in her eyes revealed a tease.

"Oh, dear." A rising tide of embarrassment heated Daisy's neck.

"Never mind. I do that all the time." Val's cheeks puffed as if to stop a loud chuckle.

"What are you ladies doing out here so early?" The sourness in Daisy's mouth made her grimace. Between the five of them, they had consumed two bottles of bubbly and the morning after wasn't pretty.

"Waiting on you." Without a crease or wrinkle on her youthful face, bright-eyed Jen, front and center, ran fingers through her glistening red highlights. At thirty-five, she was several years younger than the rest of the troupe.

"It's time for breakfast." Allison and Val spoke in unison.

Fiona gave Daisy a huge hug regardless of her appearance.

"Give me five minutes." Daisy stepped back. Affection was not something she was used to, yet the sensation of love from these ladies changed the blush of discomfort to one of joyful acceptance.

"Meet us in the dining room. We'll save a place for you," Jen said.

“Thank you.” These women were so different from her co-teachers. Daisy had done whatever she thought might work to be accepted by those she had labored with, yet never received the slightest affirmation in return. She never knew whether she would hear them backstabbing or wanting some kind of favor.

The group left, and a symphony of giggling echoed behind them down the hall and around the corner.

Daisy closed the door and went into the bathroom. After a quick shower, she brushed her teeth and donned a pair of jeans and a loose fitting orangey-yellow cardigan. Somehow she had managed to keep Pillow away from the sweater. At least she wasn’t wearing something that looked like a yeti the first day.

Daisy pulled the fob from the slot next to the door that shut off the electricity. Once breakfast was over she would return for her notebook and pen.

Her computer would have to wait until this evening when she would have time to sit and compose a few sentences. Daisy looked at the machine longingly, wooing it with a glance in hopes that some wonderful idea would write itself as she ate breakfast with the girls. Closing the door, she knew she would have better luck with a genie popping out of a lamp and granting three wishes.

The clatter of dishes and cutlery reached her even before she entered the dining room. Meals prepared for a hundred attendees was no small feat, although the summer event usually had triple the numbers.

Aroma of eggs, bacon and other breakfast items blended into a sensory-filled, mouth-watering atmosphere. Food options and portions were generous, and Daisy always went home with larger love handles as a reward.

"Yoo-hoo." Fiona waved from a table the group had ensconced in the far right-hand corner.

"Here's your place once you have your food from the self-service line." Allison pointed to a chair near the end of the table. Daylight glinted off her glasses and hid her pretty jade-green eyes. Quieter, and a tad more serious than the others, she wore her heart on her sleeve and was always on the lookout for how she could serve.

Daisy opted for a bowl of hot porridge with currants and honey instead of the full-English breakfast on offer. There would be plenty of opportunities for her to consume one in the days to come.

"So what class are you ladies going to this morning?" Jen asked, as Daisy sat and Allison poured each a cup of coffee.

"I understand some of the regulars are leading the lectures." Val cut a Cumberland sausage into small bites and smeared a piece through an egg yoke before eating it.

"Apparently Detective Superintendent Sam Decker wasn't expected to come, but was able to make it at the last minute," Fiona said.

"Barbara Bloom, the forensic specialist, is here. I went to hers last year. She was so-so. Nothing to brag about." The honey in Daisy's oatmeal melted into tiny golden ringlets.

"I'm looking forward to hearing Katharyn Cutter, the professional crime scene videographer. She and that specialist in pharmaceutical drugs, Emma Littleport, are teaching. I missed their lectures last time but heard they were excellent." Val finished her eggs and sausage and sat back with the satisfied look of a contented customer.

"There're so many wonderful choices." Allison poured another round of coffee.

"I understand they've added extras. A class on poetry. Children's books. Non-fiction topics."

"What were they thinking? It's supposed to be for crime writers." Allison collected the plates and placed them at the end of the table.

"They wanted to offer other options for those who want to come but aren't interested in murders."

"Who's *not* interested in death?" Fiona giggled and was joined by a chorus of chuckling.

"There are workshops on self publishing and social media, too."

Val moaned. "What an oxymoron. There's no such thing as media that's social. But I guess it's the only way to market books and let others know about a wonderful up-and-coming writer in their midst."

"I've decided." Allison sipped her coffee.

Everyone turned toward the normally quiet one of the bunch. "What?"

"I'm going to DS Decker's lecture. He's a bit of all right."

"That's what class I'll attend. But not because he's good looking." Daisy patted Allison's hand in assurance that finding one of the lecturers attractive was perfectly acceptable. Everyone had a favorite.

"I want to hear what he has to say, too, of course." Allison blushed.

"I'm going to my bedroom to get my things and I'll see you in the class." Daisy gulped the last of the coffee and collected her things.

"See you later. Over lunch." Jen waved goodbye, and chatter continued around the table.

Soft snowflakes fell as if downy feathers had been

accidently spilled by angels in a heavenly pillow fight.

Daisy allowed the tiny bits of plumage to land on her eyelashes and face. She might be getting old enough that Methuselah would want to dance the night away with her, but inside she skipped like a child. With friends to enjoy, life was indeed worthy of celebrating.

Her computer sat in the same place as before and glowed with radiance. No new words appeared on the screen. Creating the next chapter in the book would have to wait, but she was determined she would complete the thing this week. If J.K. Rowling could compile a manuscript in a restaurant, surely she could finish her masterpiece in this idyllic setting.

Daisy collected her notebook and pen. Murder Investigation 101 taught by the rather dapper DS awaited.

CHAPTER 4

Chairs were helter-skelter in the room and DS Decker clipped on his mike. A large white lab coat and yellow police crime scene tape were on display in a corner as props.

Daisy sat nearest the door. A quick escape just in case. Six hours stuck in an elevator in Macy's in New York years before had permanently seared claustrophobia into her brain.

Allison waved at her. "Come up front with us." Next to Allison sat a beautiful young woman. Was she a new recruit?

Even with a friend nearby, Daisy needed the freedom to leave should that specter of fear rear its ugly head. She smiled, shook her head and mouthed, "No, thank you."

The detective cleared his throat and the rumble of chatter ceased. He stepped off the short platform. "We are about to embark on a heinous crime. And as my pseudo-sergeants you are going to help solve it."

Daisy flipped her new notebook open, pen at the ready. A tingle ran down her fingers. The teacher within anticipated a lesson was about to begin and she was more than ready.

Another woman two rows over opened a laptop and began to click keys.

Tsk. Didn't the computer-bonehead read the conference brochure? *Computers are not permitted in classrooms, as they are a distraction to others who don't use them.* There was always one who had to push the envelope. At least a dozen people stared at the woman angrily, but to no avail. She tapped away with determined fingers as the detective began to pace. Detective Decker seemed oblivious to the distraction. With a remote, he flicked on the overhead, and a PowerPoint of a crime scene appeared. "It was the perfect set-up. A group of seniors were together at a getaway when one was hit with a blunt instrument. Why would anyone kill someone who seemed so innocent? Any guesses?"

Hands flew upward.

A gentleman, completely bald and quite large,

shouted, "Maybe it was a group effort. The seniors were bored and wanted something to occupy their time."

"That's silly, Charles Bond." The woman, seemingly his wife, sitting next to him elbowed his ribs.

"No answer is beyond the realm of possibility. Everyone's opinions need to be shared without comment." Detective Decker kindly chided.

The pseudo-sergeants, as DS had called them, ping-ponged ideas but Daisy kept silent. Trying to compete with the others was impossible.

The conversation evolved into a life of its own, like playing a game of Cluedo—otherwise known as Clue in America. Jen had informed Daisy at the last conference that a Mr. Pratt from Birmingham created the murder mystery game for six players. Her entire life, she had thought the game was made by Milton Bradley.

Daisy glanced at her watch. Nearly noon. Where had the time gone?

"We will continue our discussion and finalize the results in our last session." The detective blackened the overhead and turned up the lights. "I will also cover the titles of each rank in the police force for your records. So, thank you for coming this morning."

Allison and her beautiful brunette sidekick rushed to the back.

"Daisy, meet June Fellows. She's an American also."

The youthful-looking woman was built like a tall, thin chair lamp with a bob-hair cut that resembled a lampshade. Her deep brown eyes were compelling and her copper skin radiant. A long-ago bible verse read by her mother when Daisy was a child popped into her head. *Neither do people light a lamp and put it under a bowl. Instead they put it on its stand, and it gives light to everyone in the house.*

Daisy managed to push the age-old jealousy beast into its proper place—away from the view of others. "Nice to meet you."

June smiled with a beam of sweet southern charm. "It's *so* wonderful to meet you. Allison was saying how special you are and that I *must* get to know you."

Although this American would be the envy of any woman, she seemed sincere and very likable.

"We're heading to lunch, June. Care to join us?" Allison asked.

"Why, I'd *love* to."

Allison led the way while Daisy and June followed.

"How'd you find out about the writing week?"

Daisy wrapped her woolen scarf another loop around her neck. The biting wind could take your breath away even the short distance from the class to the dining room.

"There was an advertisement in the University news."

"Are you a student?"

"Yes, ma'am. I attend London University in an exchange program."

"I'm surprised you aren't in the states enjoying a family vacation."

June looked away. "I so wanted to go."

"What happened?" If Daisy had family to return to, she'd be on the next flight out of Heathrow.

"It's really expensive this time of year, and I only have two weeks off. I'd rather save my money and go during the summer when I have more time and the tickets aren't so much. How about you? Why aren't you in the states?"

"I live here. This is home now."

"No family?"

"None." Daisy nodded toward Allison. "These ladies are my family. You won't meet a nicer bunch."

"I'm looking forward to getting to know them."

They neared the dining room where a long line waited for the doors to be opened. Jen, Val and Fiona waited midway along the hallway.

Daisy, Allison and June joined the trio, as the doors to the dining facility were unlatched. The crowd shuffled forward and their ensemble was swept along with the rest as June was introduced to the others.

Allison secured a table large enough for them to sit together.

"Hey, June." A very irresistible man, around the same age as June sauntered up and wiggled his way closer. His urbane British mannerisms and suave inflection of voice would make even a stouthearted feminist faint.

"Why, Mr. Shanks. I do declare we seem to keep running into each other." June's cheeks glowed cherry-red and her accent deepened with Scarlett O'Hara charm.

"Would you mind if I joined you?"

"I'm sitting with these ladies."

Jen giggled. "He can sit at our table anytime he wants."

"Please let me introduce Mister William Shanks."

"Nice to meet you." Jen and Fiona elbowed each other and winked.

Daisy picked up a tray and stepped up to the self-serve counter. Grilled fish, scalloped potatoes with mixed vegetables, and chili were hot menu choices. Sandwiches and crisps the cold option. A hot bowl of chili sprinkled with cheese and a dollop of crème fraiche on top was a perfect choice on a raw, wintry day. A large bap with butter completed Daisy's lunch.

The group settled into chairs around the long table. June and William sat next to each other, and whispered and giggled like two young lovers.

A tiny beast of envy released its sharp claws again within Daisy. She longed for someone to share secrets and hold hands. Yet she couldn't be too upset. She was part of this female family. She smiled at the sweet couple and June nodded toward her and smiled in return.

"Will you go back this afternoon to the detective's session?" Allison asked.

"Of course. Aren't you?" Daisy turned toward her.

"I'm not sure. I'm too distracted by the chatter. I'd rather he teach than let everyone else talk."

"You've a point. But, this afternoon should be different. Anyway, I'll give you my notes if you choose to go to another class."

"Thank you. That would be lovely." Allison gathered the used cutlery and piled them on one plate.

"Anyone having a pudding?" Fiona asked.

Petite and pretty Fiona could eat a thousand puddings and not put on an ounce.

"Absolutely," Jen said as she, Val and Fiona rose.

Daisy glanced at her waistline and imagined the muffin top spilling over her jeans. "I'd rather die than say no, especially if they have sticky toffee pudding with caramel sauce on offer."

CHAPTER 5

"What's going on?" Daisy joined her friends gathered around the coffee and tea trolley where biscuits and brownies accompanied a choice of hot drink. She added milk and sugar to a mug, dropped in a Lady Grey teabag, hot water and stirred.

Mid-afternoon breaks were a quick time for a catch up, find out what the others had learned and swap notes. But this buzz of chatter was different somehow.

"I can't believe they let little Junie get the part." Fiona stomped, hands on hips. A film of anger clouded her usually cheerful countenance.

"What are you talking about?" Jen joined them, coming in late from her session. "What've I missed?"

"They had the try-outs for the Play to Stage right

after lunch and Fi didn't get the part she hoped for." Allison laid a sympathetic hand on Fiona's shoulder. "If it's any comfort, I thought you should've had it. You did fab."

"I can't imagine standing up in front of a crowd." Val stepped up next to Allison. "You were brave even to try." It was like a football team in the locker room after a loss, players giving each other the good-old boy encouragement and pat on the back.

"She only got it because of those long legs and cutesy smile...and that fake *southern* drawl." If Fiona's head were a kettle, her ears would be whistling out steam.

"What's the Play to Stage anyway? Is that something new?" Daisy chose a small piece of brownie. If she couldn't resist, she could at least cut the calories in half.

"They used to do it years ago, then stopped because they didn't have enough volunteers to help read through the submissions. Those in charge picked it up again this year."

"I guess I didn't see that in the brochure. There's so much information to absorb. What's it all about?"

"Before the conference, several attendees submit a play or story that can be performed on stage. It's extremely difficult to be chosen so the writing has to be superb. Then others get to perform. That's tough competition, too."

"Why's it so important to you?" Daisy reached for another piece of brownie. The small one merely gave cravings for more.

"Because it meant a free ticket to next year's conference. Otherwise I won't be able to come."

"You mean, if you were chosen for the part you could come without paying *anything*? I had no idea." And if she had known, she would have gladly given it a try. A teacher's retirement pay was pennies.

"With two girls getting ready to be married, we can't afford something frivolous like this..." Fiona's head of steam melted into a faucet of tears.

"Now. Now. Please don't cry." Daisy shoved the rest of the brownie into her cheek, hamster style, put an arm around her friend, squeezed and released. Brits were not necessarily known for a warm embrace even though their friendships ran deep.

"I'm so angry I swear I could do something dreadful to her." Fiona growled as she nodded toward June who entered the break area with William. June seemed oblivious to the emotional stir she caused as she waved at them from a distance with a smile the length of Route 66.

"Shhh. Someone might overhear you," Jen said.

"I don't care. She stole what I wanted."

"She didn't steal anything. She won fair and square, didn't she? Okay, maybe she has the good looks that could charm a snake, but maybe she's a good actress."

"Gee. Thanks, Jen." Fiona held the teacup close to her mouth and glared at June with venomous intent.

"You know what I meant. I'm just trying to help." Jen's youthful smile shifted into a frown. Shared pain spread across everyone's faces. You hurt one, you hurt all.

Fiona lowered her cup. "I know. Let's drop it. We need to share our notes and return to class."

Each opened a notebook and gave a quick synopsis. Allison, Val and Jen had gone to Katharyn Cutter's class on crime scene photography. Fiona went to Emma Littleport's presentation of pharmaceutical drugs after the Play to Stage try-outs although she hadn't taken too many notes. Anger at her loss came at a price for the rest of them.

Allison glanced at her watch. "It's time to get back to class."

The women dispersed. Fiona stood her ground and glowered at June as she and William walked through the crowd and left by a side door.

"Come on, Fi. It's not worth it." Daisy urged with a little tug on Fiona's elbow.

"It was worth it to me. She'll pay. Believe me, she'll pay." Fiona grabbed her things and left.

There was nothing like a woman scorned. It didn't matter if it was by a man or another woman. Revenge could clutch at the gut and not let go. Daisy swept up her notebook and headed to the third session on investigating a murder. Seemed Fiona was willing to commit one of her own.

DAISY SNUCK in and managed to find the last unoccupied chair in the back row of her class.

DS Decker paced the platform and used PowerPoint again to recap the crime scene from earlier in the day. The first session, right after breakfast, had set the stage for the crime committed against a senior while on a getaway. The second part of the class, right after lunch, had covered police ranks and a handful of laws to bear in mind when writing about crime.

"Why would anyone kill someone at a senior center?" The detective picked up where he had left off in session one. "Because one of the most convenient places to hide is in plain sight. Mr. Robinson, the dead man, was a Mafia kingpin who had cosmetic surgery done to make himself look old.

But those who knew his tricks knew how to find him."

"So who did it?" June asked from the front row.

"Always look at the people closest to the murder victim. It's a general known fact that eighty percent of those murdered knew their killers and sixteen percent were related."

"Was it a person from another mob?" Someone shouted.

"No. But that's a good guess." The detective moved toward his props. The yellow crime scene tape was an ominous reminder that killings still occurred in spite of the fact that guns were not allowed in Great Britain. Criminals found other means to take care of their prey regardless of the law.

"In this case it was the wife. He had left her high and dry. She knew that he was worth millions and if she could get rid of him she'd be set for life. So she hired someone to do the job."

"Goes to show marriage can be brutal," a man yelled from the audience. Giggles erupted.

Daisy closed her notebook. Goes to show how deep revenge can plunge into one's psyche. Fiona was angry, but was she really upset enough to do something to June? *Nah.* Fi was too sweet underneath to want to harm anyone, wasn't she?

The class finished and several dozen folks surged to the front to speak to the detective. Daisy examined him from the distance. Decker was rather attractive in a rough kind of way. She sighed. If only she could have been married. Then again, maybe she didn't want to chance nuptial bliss if someone could turn around and snuff out her life without thinking twice about it. Singleness had its own comfort. That and a good brownie went a long way.

CHAPTER 6

The blood spatters along the marble floor glittered in the moonlight like a string of beautiful rubies. The globs of moisture seemed to pulse with life from the now lifeless corpse of the victim slumped at her feet...

Daisy backspaced and deleted the word victim. What would work better? Her villain was certainly no victim. In her imagination, he deserved the imposed demise by the righteous heroine in the story. She checked the thesaurus for a replacement. Loser.

...the now lifeless corpse of the loser slumped at her feet.

That didn't sound right either. At this rate it would take twenty years for her to compose a full-length novel.

Daisy shrank the work in progress to the corner of the screen, scrolled through Facebook and updated her profile page on Twitter and LinkedIn. Everyone in the publishing world said she had to have a presence on social media. At her age, trying to create a presence was like asking Elvis to come back to life and become a contestant on America's Got Talent.

Daisy was tired of carrying on a conversation with this inanimate object called an Apple. She'd rather be eating a Granny Smith than trying to figure out what to do with Steve Jobs' brainchild.

Ring. Ring.

She sprang out of the chair.

"Hello?" Daisy glanced at the spiral circling the computer screen. The red splotches gave her an idea.

"Were you taking a kip?"

"A what?"

"A nap."

"No. Who is this?"

"Fiona. Are you coming?"

"To what?"

"The dress-up. It's Western theme, remember?"

"Oh, I forgot. But I wasn't planning on it."

"Why not? It'll be brill."

"I didn't bring anything fancy to wear. Besides I'm trying to develop a presence."

"A what?"

"Never mind." Daisy needed to brand herself. Create a faux personality. One that would draw readers to want to buy her books.

"You don't need a costume. Plus everyone's waiting on you."

"What are they doing at this thing tonight?" Maybe she could create a fake name as J.K. had done with her crime fiction using Robert Galbraith instead of Rowling. Daisy could call herself Richard Simmons. What was she thinking? That wouldn't work.

"They're having karaoke. Line dancing. Wine."

"Wine? Now you're speaking my language. I'll be there in about twenty-minutes."

"Wonderful. See you in a few." Fiona hung up.

Daisy patted the top of the computer. "All I ask is that you behave yourself while I'm out tonight. Better yet, why not step up to being the machine that has supposedly taken over the world and figure out a new name for me. Something glitzy and glamorous that makes me sound, hmm…skinny and gorgeous." Maybe she could use June Fellows? *Nah*. That name was already taken.

The spirals disappeared with a flash and the machine switched off.

THE STROBE-LIT LIBRARY had been transformed into the Old West. Bandanas were draped over hay bales and cardboard cutouts of saloon doors were propped up in three corners. Two rows of line dancers, right out of a John Wayne movie, completed the scene.

A woman in a full ruffled traditional prairie skirt that hit just below the knee was leading the pack. The man behind her wore form-fitted jeans, plaid shirt and bolo tie with braided leather and decorative metal tips secured with a large ornamental clasp.

Each dancer seemed to try and outdo the other in their lavish garb. Daisy would look like a daft cow—otherwise known as an idiot—if she tried to wear an outfit so outrageous.

An announcer walked the dancers through the moves. "Take four steps to the left with a shuffle, a kick ball change with your left foot, followed by your right foot. Pivot turn to the left, move those hips in tune to the music."

At the end of the dance line, June Fellows and William Shanks threw back their heads and laughed at each misstep.

Clapping, stomping and twirling made Daisy's head spin.

Fiona wore a bright pink cowgirl hat covered in sparkles and held a large bottle of white wine. "Have some wine."

Allison lined up the glasses on the counter in the shape of a ten-pin bowling rack and Fiona filled each halfway.

"Thanks. I wills" Daisy shouted over the music. "Better yet give me the whole bottle. This music is giving me a headache."

"Let's go into the foyer. It's not as loud out there."

Daisy, Val, Jen, Allison and Fiona picked up their glasses and headed to a quieter corner where they still had a view of the party.

"June and William are enjoying themselves." Daisy gulped the wine and held it out for Fiona to refill.

"Seems like a romance is in full bloom in our crime world."

In the other room, William placed his arm around June's waist and swung her with the finesse of Patrick Swayze.

Jen cupped her chin in her palms and sighed as she watched them dance. Allison straightened the tablecloth and rearranged the centerpiece. Fiona uncorked another bottle and Val swayed in her seat to the music.

Four bottles later, and the party began to clear. The line dancers huddled in corners and chatted. Those responsible for cleanup began the task of clearing up straw and folding away the saloon doors.

"It's time I headed to bed." Daisy wobbled as she rose. The strobe lights continued to spin even though the music had stopped and the room seemed to whirl.

"Can you get to your bedroom by yourself?" Jen giggled.

"Of course I can." Did Daisy actually slur her words?

"We can walk you back," Allison offered.

"I'll be fine."

"Why don't we go together? We're all in the same building," Fiona said.

"Don't stop your party on account of me. I'll be okay." Daisy weaved and bumped into a table.

"Ladies, we should accompany our friend." Val stood.

"Tsk. Tsk. I'm okay. Really." Daisy waved her hands in the air. "Please don't worry. What can happen from here to there? It's only a matter of minutes to get there."

"If you're sure." Jen's smooth, pretty face creased with concern.

"Honest. I'm fine." Daisy left the group of ladies and stepped out into the cold night air. A chill ran up her trouser legs, shivered along her spine and reached the nape of her neck as if she'd stepped into a huge bucket of ice.

She sprinted into the building, unlocked the bedroom door and managed to find the bed. Without changing into her nightgown she pulled back the covers and climbed in.

Just as she was about to fall asleep, the computer flicked on and the blood-red circles spiraled across the screen.

The room transformed into an amusement park tilt-a-whirl. Daisy jumped up and ran into the bathroom. She really shouldn't have had that last bit of wine.

CHAPTER 7

Daisy lurched up and made it into the bathroom again just in time. She'd rushed headlong in there three times throughout the night. Any alcohol or food should surely be out of her system by now. Obviously not.

She was not used to imbibing. Why had she done it? As the boat-rocking sensation lingered, the question mocked with insidious repetition. Why had she done it? The last time she had too much to drink was in junior high. With Lucy Lakewood. Her BFF.

Daisy sat on the edge of the bed and held her head. It felt detached from the rest of her body. She and Lucy had found a bottle of Amaretto in Lucy's house. The sweet, almond flavored liqueur tasted like dessert.

She threw ice-cold water on her face and neck.

Her reflection said it all. The wild-Jane-in-the-jungle look and disheveled hairdo would frighten Medusa. She blinked and Lucy Lakewood's image appeared in the mirror. Their parents used to say they looked like twins.

Lucy and Daisy had taken the Amaretto to the park and finished half before they realized how it affected them. That day was etched in her mind forever. Daisy had been grounded for two weeks and was actually grateful for the reprieve in her bedroom. But her parents' firm rebukes and looks of disappointment stayed with her for years.

Brushing her teeth, she spat out the foul taste that remained. Then brushed again. Damp fingers through her bedraggled hair helped tame the wild beast.

Fresh air. That's what she needed. Daisy went into the room and peeked around the window curtain. No other writers were to be seen at 0730 after a night in the Wild West. Snow fell in large nuggets and meringue-topped rocks along the walkway resembled a row of cupcakes.

Daisy put on her clothes, coat, scarf and gloves, and slipped on a pair of boots. She was ready to face the bitterness. Ice crystals dangled like earrings off the building's ledge. Winter's kiss of death seeped into her skin, and she shivered in spite of her layers.

What in the world did the British wear on their first Mount Everest expedition in 1921? They certainly didn't have the thermals of Under Armor.

The tiny lights draped along the eaves still blinked. Someone had obviously forgotten to turn them off the night before—a night of frivolity and too much wine. Daisy pushed away the thought.

She scooped a handful of snow and mashed it into a ball. She and Lucy used to pretend they were snow queens as they built snowmen and igloos. Tossing the ball, it landed with a silent plop along the edge of the lake that abutted the property. In her younger days, she might have pitched it well into the water. But, like the rest of her body, her arm wasn't what it used to be. Time and gravity hadn't been kind.

The path around the half-frozen water was still visible beneath the powder. Daisy kicked the white stuff and puffy clouds flew upwards.

Fresh air proved to be medicinal. Her blood began to flow and brain cells popped into action.

Today was a new day to attend another class. Maybe she'd go to Barbara Bloom's, the forensic specialist's, seminar. The description in the catalog made it quite a viable option. *As a specialist in forensic science, Ms. Bloom will help students examine and evaluate physical evidence as well as discuss how the use of chemicals, microscopes and physical methods are used in analyzing data.*

Daisy picked up her pace and circled around the far side of the lake. She was ready to tackle the computer again, too. Maybe during the scheduled morning break. Her novel was still in skeletal form, but she was ready to add some muscle and sinew.

The temperature seemed to drop with each of her steps as she blew into cupped hands. In the distance, a sparkly pink object bounced in the water. As out of place as a flamingo in a duck pond, the funny shaped top had familiar form.

At the edge of the bank, she drew as near as possible. The last thing she wanted was to plunge into the water and get dragged under.

Whatever it was skimmed the surface as if it skated back and forth. If only the water was frozen, she might be able to step close enough and snatch it.

She cupped her hands around her eyes to block the glare. Was that Fiona's cowboy hat? How did it get out there?

Daisy found a stick, stretched it out over the water, and hooked the object. It seemed to snag on something.

She tossed the weak limb and went in search of a larger branch. Another circle around the lake and

Daisy discovered a dead piece of wood that sat haphazard under a large, bare-leafed tree.

Daisy stretched, looped the wood under the pink hat's rim and tugged. *Ugh.* The hat snapped from whatever held it in its clasp, pole-vaulted through the air and landed on the other side of the path.

As she began to do an about-face to retrieve the flying saucer, something else bobbed to the surface.

She let out a blood-curdling scream.

A body, face down, arms outstretched and legs splayed bobbed to the surface. Bright blue fabric swayed in the water's slight tide as if the person slow danced with some unseen partner below.

Daisy slipped and caught herself just before sliding into the water's lair and let out another scream.

With little control over her legs, she pushed away, skidded over the wet surface and fell on her backside.

A shadow flitted near the tree.

"Hello? Is anyone there?" She shouted, but the dark silhouette disappeared with a passing breeze. Perhaps it had been her imagination.

"Help!" Her shout boomeranged. "Help!"

With both hands she pushed off the ground and ran the rest of the way to the building where she knew friendly faces waited.

Daisy entered the front door and bent over to catch her breath with her palms on her knees. If she weren't careful, she'd either vomit again or faint.

About to stand upright, a hand clasped her shoulder and a scream echoed in the cavernous foyer.

CHAPTER 8

Detective Decker draped a blanket over Daisy's shoulders and guided her to a chair. "Are you all right?"

She shivered from the top of her soaked hair to her wet-booted feet. "There's…there's…"

"Yes?" He knelt down beside the chair, removed her gloves, held her hands and rubbed the cold away with gentle, circular strokes. "What is it? Miss…?" His wide eyes resembled Cadbury Chocolate Buttons.

"My name's Daisy McFarland. There's a body in the lake." She pointed outside.

He bolted upright. "What? Where? Are you certain?"

If it hadn't been for some dead corpse in the water,

Daisy would have clamped onto his hands and begged him to continue to rub. It had been a long time since a man had held her so tenderly. The sensation of skin on skin was quite therapeutic and sensual.

The detective made a quick call on his mobile and ran outside. Barbara Bloom and Katharyn Cutter seemed to come from nowhere and rushed out the door behind him. Daisy recognized them from the photo ops in the catalogue. Ms. Bloom was less than professional as she dashed out still wearing plaid flannel jams and Wellington boots.

Daisy pulled the blanket closer, trying hard to calm down, but she couldn't stop shaking.

Fiona walked along the hallway, glanced at Daisy, and stopped mid-step.

"What in the world is going on?" She rushed to Daisy's side. "Are you okay?"

Daisy's teeth chattered, and her words came out in short, choppy sentences. "Are you just? Coming in? Or leaving?"

"I was out for a walk. Up toward the main road. But what's happened to you?"

"I was. Walking. Around the lake."

"And?" Fiona knelt beside her. "What in the world's going on?"

"I saw. A body in it." Daisy squeezed her eyes shut

to rid the picture from her mind but it seemed glued to the inside of her eyelids.

Fiona got up and turned as if to leave.

"W-where. Are. You going?"

"To see." Fiona shrugged with nonchalance as if she'd been told that a deer had been spotted in the woods. "Since this is a crime writer's week, it's probably just a hoax."

"Do you really think so? What a cruel joke if it is." She exhaled in relief.

"Just think about it. It's a great way to get the juices flowing and our minds to create. Bring in a dummy and throw it into the water."

Daisy stopped shaking. "That was a mean trick to play, but at least it wasn't real." The picture in her mind's eye disappeared.

"Of course it wasn't real."

"Your hat was out there. You aren't involved in the stunt, are you?" Daisy gave a nervous giggle that came out more like a gurgle.

A puzzled look washed over Fiona's features.

Detective Decker and his two sidekicks rushed back into the foyer. "We need to get the police here. Now. There's a crime scene that needs to be secured."

Fiona chuckled and looked at Daisy who joined in the laughter. "What a great idea. Call the police."

"What in the world's wrong with you two? Didn't you hear me?"

"It's a prank, right?" Fiona asked.

"This is no prank, ladies. There's a dead body out in the lake, and we need to get the authorities here as quick as possible." He hit three digits on his phone—most likely 999—reported what happened in the same professional way he had led the Murder Investigation class and hung up.

Fiona stopped laughing.

Daisy hugged the blanket closer as the shuddering began anew.

Barbara Bloom and Katharyn Cutter hurried down the hall, probably going to get warmer clothing.

"So it isn't a sordid game someone played?" Daisy got up and left a puddle on the chair. If she didn't know better, she would have thought she wet her pants.

"No. It's not." DS Decker placed his arm around her. "But it's all right, Miss McFarland. You must take it easy. You've had quite a shock."

Allison and Val came around the corner. The surprise on Allison's face when she witnessed the detective with his arm around Daisy resembled a high school girl who stumbled upon a couple making out under the bleachers.

"Well, well, well, what's going on here?" Allison asked, her eyebrows raised.

"Daisy found a dead body. A real one." Fiona glanced from woman to woman.

"Where?" Val stepped up to Daisy and the detective.

"In the lake." DS Decker squeezed Daisy's shoulder as if to keep her from falling.

The urge to feign a fainting spell and fall into his arms came from selfish motives. It had nothing to do whatsoever with the floating corpse. But Daisy straightened, moved away from his grasp and handed the blanket to him. DS Decker surely would not be attracted to a limp, weak woman.

"Who is it?" Daisy asked him. "Do you know?"

"I've no idea. But it will be a challenge to retrieve it. The weather has gotten worse and it's difficult to see, let alone reach the body without someone falling into the frigid water. Maybe there's a rowboat locked in the shed that's at the top of the drive."

"What did the police say?" Val asked, eyes wide with admiration.

Jen entered the hall. Dull daylight through the window shimmered over her hair and created a cinnamon-colored halo. "What have I missed? I was getting ready to corral everyone for breakfast but looks like you're already together. By the way, has anybody seen June?"

"Can't say I have. And I'm glad of it." Judging by her grimace, Fiona still fumed over the Play to Stage fiasco.

Jen caught sight of Daisy. "Goodness, you look as though you're soaked to the bone."

"I-I fell in the lake, and—"

"There's been a terrible accident. Or...a *murder,*" Allison said, as she approached Jen and put a hand on her shoulder ready to comfort.

"That's impossible. Who could it be?"

"We've no idea. The police are supposed to be on their way."

Detective Decker's phone rang. "Yes? I understand. Of course." His furtive glance caught Daisy's. "I'll take care of it. Thank you."

"What's wrong?" she asked.

"Seems every major road is closed. A multi-vehicle accident has shut down the M6 and the A roads are virtually at a standstill. It will be some time before help arrives." The detective brushed a hand down along his face.

"What are we going to do?" The shock of the situation finally hit Daisy, and she slumped into the wet chair.

"Oh, my." Allison gathered the women around her like a mother hen.

"Who do you suppose it is?" Fiona asked.

"At least we're accounted for." Jen sighed and held Val's elbow.

"What do we do in the meantime?" Daisy whispered, acutely aware that this week would never be the same again.

"We have the resources we need right here." Decker reassured them. "We need to secure the crime scene and identify, collect and preserve the physical evidence."

"What else?"

"We'll need to gather everyone in the main conference building. You ladies could help with that if you wouldn't mind."

"Of course," they chimed.

"Then we will develop an interrogation room where we can gather information and interview each participant on their whereabouts. Fortunately, we have these professionals gathered here so we are already well ahead of the game." He nodded toward Cutter and Bloom who had changed and now walked along the hall into the foyer.

"Do we know whether it's just a terrible tragedy?"

"Once we remove the corpse, we will have Ms.

Bloom examine it. She had already determined when we were outside that she would prepare the walk-in refrigerator in the kitchen to preserve the body until help arrives. When it will arrive, though, nobody knows."

"If it wasn't an accident—" Fiona sat on the armchair next to Daisy.

"Then there's a murderer in our midst," Jen squealed.

"Let's not draw any conclusions. What I can say is that we must be vigilant and not drop our guard. In the meantime, we need to get to work. We have a crime to solve, ladies. And it's up to us to figure out what's happened or who did this." Detective Decker slipped his phone into his pocket and did an about-face. The teacher was now the skillful expert in the criminal world. And the rest of them were front and center. No PowerPoint needed.

CHAPTER 9

"I've got to change." Daisy shook excess water from her clothes.

"We'll begin gathering everyone in the conference room." Allison offered.

"I'll meet you there in a few minutes."

"And we'll check for a means to retrieve the body." The detective, followed by Ms. Bloom and Ms. Cutter, headed toward the door.

Everyone scrambled from the foyer like a cluster of cockroaches fleeing light.

Daisy went to her bedroom, towel-dried her hair, made a quick superman-in-the-phone-booth change, and rushed back to the now empty foyer. Activity, then silence. Life, then death. The paradox was not lost on her. The wet seat she had used was still imprinted with her bottom. Water spots marred the otherwise clean hardwood floor.

A yellow slip of paper about the size of a post-it-note protruded from beneath the chair and caught Daisy's attention. She picked it up, scanned the telephone number scribbled on it, pushed the note into her coat pocket and dashed toward the conference room. Although she'd been on her own most of her life, being alone right now scared her more than she'd ever known.

THE DRONE of voices hovered over the opened area. A separate building from the rest, it was a makeshift theater, music-practice studio, and artist workspace for attendees.

Daisy, breathless and lightheaded, entered. The main section had an artery of smaller rooms that could be closed for private use or personal reflection. Each morning a time for meditative contemplation was offered in one of them.

She scanned for Fiona, Val and the others, caught the red in Jen's hair and weaved her way to the far side.

"There you are." Allison raced up to Daisy and pulled her along. "We were worried about you."

Claustrophobia began to squeeze her throat as the crowd folded in. Daisy swallowed long and hard. "I can do this. I can do this," she murmured.

"Are you okay?" Val asked.

"I'll be fine. What have I missed?" Daisy was surrounded wagon-circle style by the ladies.

"Nothing yet." Fiona fiddled with her purse, pulled out a lipstick tube and rubbed it across her lips. Her hands shook and the tube slipped, leaving a small glossy red streak alongside her chin. She rubbed it away with the backside of her hand.

A tap on the mike, and the drone of noise ceased. Detective Decker tapped again. "Is this on?"

"Yes, sir." The technician waved from the back. "It's hot."

"Ladies and gentleman," the detective cleared his throat.

"What's happened? Who's been murdered?" The large man from the Murder Investigation Class shouted. His wife ribbed him. "Be quiet, Charles."

"Right now we are still determining the cause of death. But to bring everyone up to date, a person was found in the lake early this morning by Ms. Daisy McFarland."

An intake of air from the crowd threatened to suck out all the oxygen. Everyone looked this way and that for the mysterious McFarland. Daisy wanted to retreat under the floorboard. But once she had been located, the crowd transferred their attention back toward the front.

"We've managed to retrieve the body and it has been taken to a large spare walk-in refrigerator where our forensic specialist will figure out what's happened."

"Where are the police? Why aren't they here?" A slim, librarian-type young woman with oversized glasses squealed as if she were going to burst into tears.

"There's no need for concern, Miss Peabody. They've been detained due to the weather and road conditions. But for the time being we have what is required to take care of this situation."

"Why are we being detained like a herd of cattle going to slaughter?" A rough character built like a monster truck with muscles pushing his shirt to the limit, clenched his fists.

"Who could that be?" Val whispered. "He doesn't look like a writer."

"He's the maintenance man," Fiona said.

"Please, sir." Detective Decker patted the air to calm the brewing storm. "This was the best way to squelch any rumors and to take statements from each of you. We won't keep you here any longer than necessary. I promise."

“Then get on with it, man.” The brute unclenched his fists.

“What I propose is that we form groups of ten. Each group will be interviewed by Ms. Cutter to find out where each of you were during the time we believe the incident occurred. When each group of ten is finished, you can move to the dining area and get breakfast. Fair enough?”

Everyone in the crowd shook their heads in unison except Mr. Brute and large Charles Bond who stood firm without expressions.

“Can you tell us who it is?” The technician asked.

“I’m not at liberty to reveal that information just yet.”

A low murmur passed through the crowd.

“Please everyone, begin forming groups of ten. Will the first group please go into that room over there.” He pointed to an area directly behind the stage. “Then each follow in sequence into the other areas. Thank you.” The detective removed the mike clip from his lapel and directed them where to go.

William Shanks shuffled his way among the moving throng and stepped up to Daisy and the rest of the ladies. “Have any of you seen June? I’ve searched for her everywhere.”

Fiona muttered, “Last I saw her she was with you

at the Western." She headed toward an empty room. "Let's go over to that one."

"May I join you?" William asked.

"Of course." Allison directed the group with the skill of an orchestra conductor. "We must stay together and take care of one another. It's what friends do."

The small retinue huddled together

"I'm hungry," Jen said.

"And I'm tired of waiting and not being told what's going on." Fiona paced the tiny area.

A few minutes later Ms. Cutter joined them. "Hello everyone. This shouldn't take too long. What I need to know is where you were this morning at approximately 0730. Ms. McFarland, we already have your details. You may leave if you wish."

Daisy glanced at the others. "I can't leave. These ladies are—" She heard the break in her voice.

"We are in this together. We're family." Fiona came between Daisy and Ms. Cutter.

"What a nice gesture. But someone has more than likely killed someone in our midst, so I would choose my companions very carefully if I were you."

The women looked at each other, and their room suddenly became a morgue of silence.

CHAPTER 10

"What a formidable challenge to have to interview everyone." Daisy's plate was loaded with a full English breakfast, toast on the side, as she pushed the tray along the self-help line.

"I felt like a criminal with those questions." Fiona filled her plate with scrambled eggs, waffles and poured syrup over the lot. "Cutter, the forensic scientist who cuts into cadavers seems a nutter. Her beady eyeballs make me wonder if she's ever attempted an assassination of some sort."

Jen stepped behind them, pushed her tray along the serving counter and smothered two pieces of toast with baked beans.

Daisy leaned across to view Jen's food. One had to have a certain type of palate to appreciate British cuisine. "What a strange breakfast entrée."

Jen looked at her plate. "It's kind of like Marmite. You either love or hate it."

Allison, next in line, filled a bowl with porridge, currants and a swirl of honey. Steam from the buffet fogged her glasses and lent a rather spooky air to her appearance. "Was Cutter trying to turn us against each other by saying we needed to be careful who we choose as friends?"

"It was a mean thing to say." Val pulled up the rear and followed Allison's lead in having porridge. "We've been mates for years and nothing has ever gone wrong."

Daisy led the group to a table they found beforehand. William, head cupped in his hands, sat in the center chair.

"Why wouldn't we trust each other?" Fiona settled into a seat and reached for the condiments.

"She was just making an observation." Allison pulled out a chair next to William and gave him a sideward glance as she sat.

"Cutter gives me the creeps. She has the knowledge anyone needs to commit a crime and no one would be the wiser." Jen reached for the pepper and shook it vigorously.

"But why would she?" Val asked.

"Who knows what causes a murderer to do what

they do? If you could answer that, there wouldn't be a need for a police department."

"You watch too many Midsomer Murders."

"So?" Jen shrugged.

Daisy rearranged the food on her plate. How could they just sit there and theorize about a homicide when one might have occurred last night? Or could it have just been a horrible accident?

"We have nothing to worry about. We just need to answer the questions and get on with the day." Allison scooped a spoon of porridge and looked at William again.

William lifted his head. "Do you suppose everyone will carry on like nothing's happened? There's a dead body in the refrigerator."

"Makes my skin crawl if you ask me." Fiona ate her last bite of waffle and chased it down with a gulp of coffee.

"Makes me not want to eat." Daisy pushed the food away. No matter how tantalizing the smell of bacon might be, there was nothing like a murder to help kill the appetite.

"I'm not sure what we're supposed to do while we're waiting on the police. We can't go anywhere, so maybe they *should* resume the schedule," Jen said.

"Should I ask the detective?" Daisy nodded toward him as he entered. She hadn't really noticed until now how muscular he was, and the dimple in his chin made him rather youthful although she assumed he had to be in his fifties.

Allison jumped up. "I'll ask."

"Me thinks our friend has a crush on someone." Jen nodded at Allison's retreating back.

"I'm really worried about June. It's not like her to miss breakfast," William said.

Allison returned to the table with DS Decker in tow. "Seems the detective would like to speak to you privately, Fi."

Fiona rose. Her forehead formed a deep V as if bewildered. "What do you want?"

"Could you please come with me?"

"Fi, do you want me to go with you?" Daisy asked.

"I'd rather you wouldn't, Ms. McFarland." One corner of the detective's mouth curled upward.

"Please let her come. Whatever you have to say, you can say in front of her." Fiona stood behind Daisy's chair.

"Very well."

The three left and the murmur of gossip followed close behind.

Daisy and Fiona followed Detective Decker to the library where it had been decorated with Old Western style paraphernalia the previous night. Now it was a makeshift interrogation room.

Four computers lined one wall and several conference attendees clicked on keyboards in what appeared a frenzied state. Perhaps they were assisting Decker in searching out details. Or maybe they were trying to reach loved ones back home with the news.

Books lined every area except the large front bay window through which Daisy noticed clumps of snow falling. Had it only been a few days ago when those same wads of white had reminded her of a heavenly pillow fight? Now they appeared ominous as prison bars to the outside world. They prevented the police from coming and any escape for those that remained on the premises.

A large table with one chair behind it and two in front occupied the middle section.

"Please sit ladies." Decker pointed to the two seats and sat on the one behind the makeshift desk. He moved a stack of folders from one side to the other, folded his hands and leaned forward.

"What's this about?" Fiona twisted her fingers and bounced her legs, but her voice was firm and controlled. She seemed to waver between fight and flight.

Daisy placed a hand on Fiona's knee to stop her nervous energy.

"I wanted to let you know that the body found was that of June Fellows."

"What?" Fiona leapt from her seat.

'"Please sit." He waved downward.

Daisy tugged gently on the edge of Fiona's blouse to urge her into the chair. "I'm sorry to hear that. She was a sweet girl. Surely it was an accident?"

"We thought so at first. Then we found a large bottle of bubbly hidden behind a bush nearby."

"That's odd. I didn't see any bottle. But of course once I saw the…the…body…well, all I wanted to do was escape and find help."

"We figured she had too much to drink and it was just an unfortunate tragedy."

"But?"

"The strange thing was that on closer examination, the bottle was full and partially frozen—and just about ready to explode."

"I'm dreadfully sorry, but what does this have to do with me? I didn't even know the girl." Fiona sat straighter, held the chair and shifted backward. She seemed in total charge again.

The detective drummed his fingers gently then

stopped. "First, a pink hat was found near the body and not far from where the bottle was found. I understand from others at the party, it was yours."

Daisy cleared her throat. "Um. Actually the hat was in the water and I pulled it out with a stick." She rushed on to explain. "I had no idea it was attached to anything."

"So you're telling me that the hat was actually tied to the body?"

"It seemed stuck at first, but when I yanked harder, it flew into the air and that's when I saw… June." Daisy wiped her sweaty palms across her thighs. Would she now be a suspect?

Decker turned toward Fiona. "It seems your hat was found *on* the body. Do you know how that happened?"

"I've no idea. I left the hoedown soon after Daisy and forgot to take it with me. Anyone could have picked it up."

"Did anyone see you leave the party without it?" He prodded.

"I'm not sure. Everyone was pretty inebriated, so why would they have noticed?"

"I understand that you had a grudge against Ms. Fellows."

"Who said that?" Fiona's chin quivered. The ice queen began to melt.

"It was no secret that you were very disappointed with the results of the Play to Stage choice. Apparently when the try-outs were over it was reported you said you would get even with the victim. I'm afraid this doesn't look very good for you."

Daisy rose, hands on hips, her voice cold and hard. "How could you possibly believe my dear friend could harm anyone? She's one of the kindest, most wonderful people I know."

"Please, Ms. McFarland. I'm not saying she had anything to do with it, but the evidence could be considered incriminating in a court of law."

Fiona collapsed forward and her shoulders heaved from an onslaught of despair.

CHAPTER 11

"That's ludicrous." Daisy placed her hands on the detective's desk, leaned forward, her face inches from his.

He pushed backward and the front legs of his chair lifted. Decker crossed his arms over his muscular chest, and the side of his mouth curled upward as it had done earlier. "For the moment I'm just gathering facts. There are no clear indications of how this crime was committed. But we must take into account the evidence we have so far."

Daisy stepped away and sat. For some reason this man disarmed her unlike any other. "I'm sure you're only trying to do your job," she said softly.

"Everyone's trying to make the most of this difficult situation, including me."

"I swear. I didn't do anything to that woman." Fiona wiped her damp cheeks with a swipe. "I was angry, but I wouldn't hurt a spider let alone another human being."

Decker turned his attention to Fiona. "I must follow every lead. I'm sorry. In the meantime, please go and finish your breakfast. I will come for you if I have any further questions."

"You mean I can leave?"

"Yes. For the time being."

Fiona bolted like a horse from a barn fire.

"I'm sorry about your friend. These things are never pleasant." The front legs of the detective's chair fell with a thump.

"Me too. Fi is a super person, and I guarantee you she wouldn't do anything but hug someone to death and then resuscitate them immediately."

The detective's mouth curled fuller this time.

"Is there anything else I can do to help? I'm not sure how. But as a retired teacher I'm pretty good at corralling misbehaving students."

"It will be in everyone's best interest if classes resume as normal. Otherwise the entire group won't know what to do with themselves. Bored people, worried if there's possibly a murderer on the loose, could create the perfect storm of unrest and anger. And right now we don't need that."

"Are the instructors able to teach since they're also helping you with the investigation?"

"We've talked about it, and we'll take shifts teaching and use our free time to continue to unravel the evidence. Nobody can leave in this raging snowstorm, so we don't need to worry about anyone taking off."

"Should we have a pseudo-policeman in each class to keep some semblance of order and be sure no one else gets hurt?"

"Grand idea. You'd make a fine police officer, Ms. McFarland." DS Decker came around the table. Daisy backed up. If she wasn't careful, the perfect storm might happen right in her stomach as his nearing presence created a swirl of butterflies a lepidopterist would envy.

DAISY STOOD on a chair at the entrance of the dining room and steadied herself when the seat wobbled as she shifted her weight. "Please everyone, may I have your attention?" It seemed impossible to get this group of adults to listen. She had better luck with a gymnasium full of students at a pep rally.

Allison rapped a glass with her fork. Jen and Val joined in. The chatter of conversation began to slow and heads turned toward Daisy. She cleared her throat. Why was it so much harder to speak to a group of peers than squawking adolescents?

"Detective Decker suggests we attend our scheduled classes." The murmur escalated to a low rumble. She waved her palms downward. "Please, everyone. We're better off staying busy. Our instructors have agreed to continue. The least we can do is support them at this time. And the best way to do that is by maintaining a routine and everyone remaining calm."

Charles Bond began to rise with a large scowl. His wife yanked his sweater and dragged him back onto his seat.

Allison stood. "Great idea, Daisy. I say we decide which one we want to attend and go there in as composed a manner as possible." Daisy smiled at her. What would she do without these ladies?

"But what if someone's out to kill us?" Miss Peabody, the wide-eyed librarian, glanced around as she tugged and twisted a strand of hair. It was as if she expected the murderer to pounce on her that very minute.

"We've discussed that and each class will have an assigned guard."

Miss Peabody sat, released a low gasp of air and relaxed.

"Do we agree?"

The majority nodded. The few naysayers kept their arms crossed. There always would be a small number in a crowd who'd disagree with any option or opinion.

Daisy stepped down, went back to the table, picked up her things and strutted out. In the hallway, she stood as the crowd filed out in an orderly manner. The sight of it made her smile. The power of one. She never imagined she would ever be *the one*.

Daisy entered the class and waited near the door as the seats began to fill. She sought an empty chair in the last row.

Emma Littleport, specialist in pharmaceutical drugs, shuffled a pile of papers into a stack at the podium. Built more like a ballerina than what Daisy imagined a scientist to look like, Emma seemed to float along the stage. "Good morning, everyone. In spite of our current difficulties, I do hope you can learn some things that will prove useful as writers. Let's begin with forensic toxicology. In 2006, twenty percent of deaths in the United States were caused by some type of drug. That statistic, of course, also includes suicides and accidental overdoses."

"Is that what happened to the person in the lake?" A man asked.

"We will not discuss any details about the ongoing investigation since we don't have any specifics as of yet on what caused this loss of life." Emma glided to the other side.

"But what if someone uses drugs to poison the lot of us? They could have put something in the porridge," shouted another person.

The persona of prima ballerina shifted to competent professor as Emma straightened her spine and clasped her hands behind her back. "We will *not* discuss this. Do I make myself perfectly clear?"

Heads nodded in agreement.

"We are here to learn so that you can present your work with professional insights that will make your stories come alive."

Two seats down from Daisy, a young man with a crew cut, torn jeans, and Converse, laughed. "No pun intended, right?"

Emma giggled and released her hands. "Exactly. Now shall we begin?" She motioned to the tech, who lowered the lights and clicked on PowerPoint. Charts of various medicines, drugs and paraphernalia were displayed. Daisy jotted notes as the instructor used a laser beam, pointed to each and talked about them as she went along.

The rest of the attendees seemed absorbed in gaining knowledge for their crime novels and for the moment put aside the unsettling scenario that had just played out.

The irony was not lost on Daisy and she was certain it wasn't lost on the others. It was possible they were discussing the very means used on the dead body that had been found floating in the semi-frozen water merely yards away from this warm place filled with potential killers.

Daisy paid close attention to every item Emma discussed. One detail could perhaps be a clue as to what had happened to June, and she was willing and able to come alongside Decker and help find the murderer in their midst.

CHAPTER 12

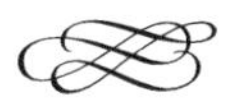

The blood splatters, that before had resembled a string of rubies, lost their luster in the fading light and now looked like blobs of ink dyed with bromine. The Loser was no longer a threat and those who had been tormented by their existence could sleep peacefully tonight. No one need worry if this beast would crawl into a window and rob them of a loved one. But was death ever justified?

Daisy had been inspired after leaving the toxicology class and returned to her bedroom. The manuscript begged attention and she coaxed words to flow from her brain to the keys.

She blew softly on a cup of Lady Grey so as to cool off the drink without spilling it. The beauty of staying anywhere in Great Britain was that a kettle and tea things were always included in the accommodations.

Daisy reread the last paragraph on the screen. Instead of a brutal blow by a blunt object, perhaps the protagonist could use some deadly nightshade —*Atropa Belladonna,* the Latin name according to Emma—and slowly poison The Loser.

She had no idea that there were so many potential, undetected poisons. Who would ever guess there was a poison-dart frog, or a blue-ringed octopus whose venom was ten times deadlier than cyanide? But the kicker was the hooded pitohui, the only known poisonous bird found in Papua New Guinea. Emma definitely knew her poisons.

If anyone ever checked the 'history' on Daisy's computer they might wonder if she wasn't responsible for June's death. Every crime writer did extensive research so anyone who attended the conference could conceal the means of committing someone's death and not be suspect.

Rap. Rap.

Daisy opened the door. DS Decker, covered with snow, lips curled upward, removed his hat and released a shower of snowflakes. He looked like one of those snow globes that when shaken unleashed falling white flakes over Frosty. "I'm sorry to bother you, Ms. McFarland."

"Please call me Daisy." Was it appropriate for her to invite the man in? After all, if anyone found out about it, it would reek of impropriety and gossip would spread like the bubonic plague.

She poked her head out the door and looked in both directions. There was no way Daisy wanted rumors flying about some kind of dalliance going on. "Please come in and dry off."

Decker stepped inside. The white covering on his coat melted within seconds and left a small pool beneath his feet. "Oops. I'm sorry."

"Don't worry. It's only wa—wa—water." Daisy needed to get a grip and not come across like a sixteen-year-old on a blind date. She threw back her small shoulders, pulled in her stomach and tucked in her bottom. "What can I do for you?"

"I wondered if you would come with me to the library?"

Cluedo popped in her mind immediately. Follow the detective to the library and find a dagger used by the maid on the Colonel.

"Is there's something wrong?" Was she now a suspect as she'd feared might happen?

"No. I have a problem and some questions."

"Oh dear. I hope your problem isn't another body?"

He tilted his head to one side. A puzzled look

replaced his curled lips and he scratched the side of his temple. "Um. No. Not another corpse."

Now why had she said that?

"It's this draft I'm writing."

He stopped scratching but his brows still creased into a frown.

"Working on my novel somehow keeps dead bodies first and foremost in my thoughts."

"Ah. Well, I guess I could see how that could happen."

Daisy knew instinctively he hadn't any idea.

"What did you want to ask me?"

"I wanted to find out more about the hat and what you actually saw when you discovered the body."

"I believe I've told you everything I know."

"Also, we believe we've uncovered some clues that are proving useful in determining whether this was in fact an accident or a homicide and I wanted your advice. As a teacher, I believe you have some insights into group dynamics and behavioral patterns."

"Why didn't you say so?" Daisy grabbed her things, wrapped a scarf around her neck, and pulled on gloves and boots before retrieving her key.

Decker opened the door and standing on the

threshold were Allison, Val, Jen and Fiona, mouths wide open.

"This isn't what it looks like—" Daisy sputtered.

"I'm sure you're right, but that's too bad if it isn't." Jen teased, and the continual glimmer in her eye twinkled brighter.

Allison lowered her lids.

Val beamed and Fiona gasped as if she'd seen a ghost when she first laid eyes on Decker.

"We were heading to the library. But if you need to take care of business beforehand, I can meet you there, Ms. McFarland. Um. Daisy." He left, his face still red.

"Daisy, now, is it?" Jen elbowed her.

"It's not like that."

"It's none of our business." Allison's pooled eyes appeared larger through her eyeglasses.

"But I want to hear more." Val inched forward. "So let's go to the lounge and chat there."

"That isn't why you came by. What's going on?" Daisy closed the door and the group made their way to the stairwell instead of the elevator. With the food they'd consumed, every step counted toward exercise.

"Our phones don't seem to be working right now. I guess there's no service because of the storm." Jen led the way.

"That's only part of the reason we came to collect you, though." Val followed behind.

"Let's be honest, we're still a little worried about being on our own." Allison walked beside Daisy.

"But you don't seemed bothered." Fiona followed last.

"You wouldn't be bothered either if you had a detective on your doorstep." Jen looked back at them and giggled.

The others joined in. Allison smiled, and Daisy knew her friend would never hold a grudge for long.

"Are you okay, Daisy?"

"What?"

"You stopped laughing suddenly. Is something the matter?"

"It's Pillow. She must be worried sick. Usually I call and check up on her every day. Somehow I've forgotten to do that and I had no idea the phones were out." In the scramble of finding June, getting the crowd into their classes and attending Emma's lesson, Daisy had totally forgot to contact Rosemary and ask about Pillow. What a horrible cat-mom.

"Could it be that handsome someone who's been keeping you busy?" Jen's twinkle brightened once more.

Daisy stopped in her tracks on a step. "Look at me. I'm retired. I'm old and I'm no one's dream of a date. So can we stop speculating about some romantic encounter taking place here?"

"Me thinks tho' protests too much."

"No, I just don't have any unrealistic expectations. Situations like these cause people to act out of character."

"So it's just the drama of what's going on that's drawing you and Deck together?" Allison asked with a whisper.

"We aren't together."

"I'm sorry."

"Don't be. It's okay. I gave up the Cinderella meets her prince and lives happily ever after a long time ago. Pillow and I are very content just as we are."

Daisy stepped down and the others followed suit. They popped out from the stairwell and walked the distance to the lounge and headed outside. There was no sound other than the crunch of frozen ground breaking beneath their feet.

CHAPTER 13

"Let me get this straight. We're going to create a chain to stay in touch with each other." Daisy finished her cocoa and placed the mug into the tray with the other used cups.

Fiona nodded.

"If we haven't heard from each other—me and Fi pairing up, and Jen, Val and Allison joining together as a team—we'll pass the word and reconvene here within thirty minutes of anyone missing."

"That's right," Allison said.

"Got it."

The ladies separated and went their own way.

Daisy went outside and gazed skyward before going into the library. Snow gems sparkled under a lamppost and caused the sensation of entering Narnia's wardrobe. C.S. Lewis was a word-magician who'd captured her imagination with *The Lion, The Witch and The Wardrobe*" and became her favorite writer.

For some strange reason, she wasn't afraid. A bit on tenterhooks, perhaps. Yet the situation seemed to center on one person. June. If there were a mass murderer, surely they would have already struck again. Daisy didn't have a criminal mind, but it seemed irrational to pick on a group of writers. Yet hadn't DS Decker talked in his class about a group of senior citizens who'd once had a murderer in their midst? But there again, there had only been one victim and it was deliberate and personal.

The white wafers spun and twisted as if they danced in some ritualistic manner to the light goddess that shone above. Many years ago, Daisy's parents had taught her about a Creator, and others might call her old-fashioned, but seeing these delicate flakes reassured her it was so.

Daisy shivered and entered the library. Hopefully, Decker was still there and hadn't given up on her.

"Good evening, Daisy." Detective Decker sat behind his faux-desk, pulled off reading glasses, and rubbed his eyes. The computer programmer desks were abandoned and only a low hum resonated from the machines.

"It's so picturesque outside, I didn't want to come in. I hope I didn't delay you leaving your makeshift police office?"

"Of course not. I'll be here until I figure this out, although I seem to have reached a stalemate."

Daisy sat on the chair across from him. "You said you had a problem. And wanted some advice?"

"It seems right after I spoke with you and Fiona earlier today something went missing from my desk." He touched the folders stacked on one corner.

"Were they of importance? Maybe someone just moved them to a safer place."

"I only wish that were so." He pulled a palm along his mouth and massaged his chin. The sparkle disappeared from his features, and was replaced with a shadow of foreboding.

"Do you think *I* might have done something with what's missing? Is that why you're asking?" Daisy's hackles ratcheted up a notch. Self-defense had always been her first fallback when feeling accused.

"No. Of course not. Be assured, I had no thought that you may have taken anything."

"Then why mention it?"

"To be honest, I'm not sure who to trust right now, and I thought perhaps you might be a sounding board. That is, if you wouldn't mind?" His brown eyes pierced hers.

"Um. Oh. Of course not." A warm sensation traveled up her neck and into her face, pleasantly smoothing her nervous hackles.

Decker released a sigh. "It would be different under other circumstances. If we were investigating a crime where I had other officers to help me, I wouldn't necessarily share with a civilian, if you will."

"I understand entirely."

"I don't really know the other instructors who're helping out. Only through our mutual teaching arrangements here do I have any idea who they are. And I can't dismiss anyone from being a suspect."

"So it's been determined June didn't have an accident?"

"I'm afraid so. Judging by what Ms. Bloom found on the body, there's too much evidence to suggest otherwise."

Daisy sat back and allowed herself a few minutes to process the news. June had been a bubbly student with the rest of her life ahead of her. Why would someone harm such an innocent girl?

"You see, the papers that we retrieved from June Fellows had some incriminating information on certain individuals here at the conference, and I dare not mention anything to anyone I deem involved."

"I understand the difficulty you're in. It's like

telling one student you think others have cheated on a test and expect them not to say anything."

"Exactly."

"What were those papers, if you don't mind me asking?"

"Obviously I can't give you details but it appears our Ms. Fellows was anything but an innocent student in London University."

Daisy straightened. "What do you mean?"

"Ms. Fellows was actually an investigative reporter and used this platform to confirm her suspicions of certain people and alleged unlawful acts they were committing. It was the perfect cover up for her to be here. And it also appears—" Decker paused and tilted his head. "Did you hear that?"

"What?" Daisy's muscles tightened across her shoulders and down her arms.

"Never mind. I must be getting a bit paranoid with this weather and inability to connect with anyone outside of the conference."

She tried to relax, but the muscles across her shoulders refused to obey. "So it appears, what?"

"As I began scanning the papers we'd found, I realized she was blackmailing those she suspected. I stepped away from the desk before reading the potential list of people she'd targeted. By the time I returned, they were gone."

"So you can eliminate Fiona from your suspects then? She's just a mom and wife, June wouldn't have any criminal activity about her." Daisy released a sigh. Others might be villains, but her friend was anything but.

"I'm afraid that's not so. I only scanned one page, but Fiona's name was on it."

"Surely you're joking?"

"No I'm not. And I ask that you don't mention this to her."

"Like the student who's been told that others have been found cheating?"

"Precisely."

"Oh, dear." Daisy loved Fiona and would do anything to clear her name. For the time being she would have to remain quiet and would continue to help the detective find the man or woman responsible.

"Do I have your word?"

"Yes. You do. Although I know this horrible crime can't involve her in any way."

"I admire your loyalty."

"And I love my friends. Fi might be reckless when it comes to opening a bottle of Prosecco, but she's not careless when it comes to decisions regarding her life and that of her family."

"Thank you. I will bear that in mind."

"So what advice were you seeking?"

"To quote a famous teacher, how do I get the students to tell on each other?"

"Ah, now that's another matter entirely especially since you've stated you don't know who you can trust. But I did have a trick up my sleeve when I used to teach. Would you care to hear it?"

Decker winked. "You bet I would."

CHAPTER 14

"Play the sympathy card," Daisy said, offering a small, mischievous smile.

"The what?"

"Sympathy. That's what I do to get students to help, hopefully without suspecting anything."

Decker laced his fingers and leaned forward. "And how do you go about doing that?"

"It's easy. And let's be honest, underneath every adult is still an elementary student who wants to be accepted by their peers."

"A compelling theory. But I believe you're correct."

"What I do is tell student *A* that their friend, student *B*, is a wonderful person who seems to be going through a difficult time."

"You lie?"

"It's more like luring or baiting in order to fish for information. Most of the time what I say is fact. *B* probably has demonstrated signs of unexplainable behavior to *A*. Of course, there are situations where I don't tell the entire truth in order to dig underneath. Perhaps find out what they find likeable in that person. Follow so far?"

"I believe so."

"When I get a student to share the things they like about their friend, I slowly shift the conversation and say I believe something might be bothering that person and maybe they could help."

Decker rose and went to a sideboard. "Coffee?"

"Thank you. But I'd better not. It'll wake me up in the night. Plus I just had some cocoa with the others."

He poured. Steam rose and lifted into a puff that quickly dissipated toward the lofty ceiling.

The detective went to the front window, looked outside a few moments, and turned to Daisy as he leaned on the window ledge. "Let me get this straight. I should go to a teacher here that might be good friends with someone else. Get them talking about that person and gradually lead the conversation to some concerns I may have."

"Sure. You could say that maybe being trapped here is starting to wear on them. What could you do to help? Have you noticed if they're acting out of character? That kind of thing. I'm sure you do this in your job without even realizing it."

"I suppose you're right."

"As a matter of fact…"

"Yes?"

"It just occurred to me that you could be playing the same mind game with me." She stood, paced a few steps and stopped in front of him.

"How do you mean?" He sipped the coffee, his expression blank.

"Perhaps you lured me to speak about Fiona. You've already been doing that whether you realized or not."

"I suppose you could see it that way." He rose from leaning on the sill and advanced toward her.

"So have you?"

"Perhaps unconsciously."

The hackles rose again on Daisy only this time they traveled up her neck and over her entire scalp as if she'd put a finger in an electric socket. Would there ever be a time she would meet someone she could trust implicitly? Had she unintentionally said anything to Decker that could be construed as negative about Fiona? She'd been so enamored by this smooth salesman that she nearly sold out Fiona to get his approval. She snatched her coat and headed to the door.

"Wait. Please."

She looked back at him.

"I'm sorry. Truly. I had no intention of stepping between you and Fiona or asking you to betray her. But I must do my job."

"And your job is using anyone in any way possible to gain their confidence. I've played the same game, Detective, and I recognize a charlatan when I see one." She stomped out and slammed the door.

STEAM ROSE from the hot water that poured from the bathroom faucet. Daisy filled the basin and washed away her tears. In the mirror, her blotched reflective look was anything but attractive. She'd been so foolish. She dried her face and hands and switched off the light.

Daisy filled the kettle and clicked it on, dropped a chamomile tea bag into a cup and snapped the curtains closed. Tears begged to be released but she forced them down with a large gulp and sat at the computer. She wasn't foolish, just downright pathetic.

She punched in her password and the blue screen popped up. Decker's imaginary face glowed from the monitor. Daisy blinked and forced those attractive brown buttons and dimpled chin to disappear.

It had been so long since someone had shown her attention, let alone wanted her opinion. She clicked on iPhoto and scrolled through pictures of Pillow when she first brought her home. They always gave Daisy a good chuckle, and she needed a major distraction right now.

Pillow's mottled fur made the kitten look like a small fox except for her rather oversized head and skinny legs. One time, she'd gotten her nose stuck in an empty toilet roll and lifted her face as if she had an elephant's trunk. The noise Pillow made had Daisy in tears with laughter.

Next she brought up a picture she'd snapped before leaving home. She caressed the screen as if to pet her little hero. Pillow would have never fallen for the likes of DS Decker. The cat was a good judge of character. Daisy had long forgotten how to judge anyone—good or bad. But this latest emotional burn would keep her from sticking fingers into a hot pot where they did not belong for quite some time.

Rap. Rap.

Daisy peered through the fish-eye lens peephole

and stared at the malformed face of Decker on the other side. She stepped back.

Rap. Rap. "I know you're in there."

"So what if I am?"

"Please open the door."

"Go away."

She waited a few minutes and looked out the lens again.

"I'm not leaving until you open the door."

"Stop shouting." Daisy yanked it open. "And go away."

Other doors along the hallway opened and several attendees poked their heads out.

Decker glanced this way and that. "Everyone please go back into your rooms. Everything's fine here."

"Is she the guilty one?" Big Charles stepped out and pointed toward Daisy. "I thought she looked suspicious." His wife dragged him back in and slammed the door.

Decker started to laugh.

Daisy propped fists on her hips and snarled, "How dare you make fun at my expense?"

The detective's face grew serious as he advanced toward Daisy, forcing her to retreat. "I'm not making fun of you. That man always makes me chuckle. There's always someone who's a better judge of character than anyone else, and they make their opinions known."

"What do you want?" Daisy sat on the desk chair and blackened the screen.

"I want to apologize."

"No apology necessary. You were just doing your job."

"In part. But I was also trying to be very honest."

"Like using a bait to lure a fish into disclosing information."

"It was nothing like that. Of course, I need to know about Fiona. But only because there are so many things that point to her. But I also know that when that happens it usually turns out that the clues were decoys to take the attention off the real criminal."

"So you don't think she's involved?" Daisy whispered.

"I don't know. But I do know that I trust you. Not that I really know you, but I've seen you around others, and you're obviously admired a great deal. And that means plenty in my book."

Her pulse raced quicker than she thought possible and she felt out of breath. As if she'd run a marathon without any training. Her? Admired?

"Are you okay?" He knelt before her. "You look like you're going to faint."

"I'm fine." She got up and moved toward the curtains.

Decker rose and swiped his knees. "Please forgive me."

"I do," she whispered.

"And would you still consider helping me? I know that might be too much to ask right now, but I honestly need a confidante."

She swallowed, afraid to speak, afraid the tears might take over and she would embarrass this man, and herself. Daisy nodded once. "Yes. I'll help but I will not say another word about Fiona. That's my only stipulation."

"Fair enough. Tomorrow then?" He stepped out and closed the door quietly behind him.

Daisy slumped into the chair and hit the enter button. Pillow's toilet-rolled nose popped up and Daisy smiled. Perhaps her cat might like Decker after all.

CHAPTER 15

"What did Decker say after you left us last night?" Allison, wide-eyed and appearing refreshed from apparently a good night's sleep, sidled up to Daisy the next morning in the class on crime scene photography.

"I'll tell you later," Daisy whispered. "Looks like we're about to begin."

Katharyn Cutter clipped the microphone onto her large-lapel, navy jacket. Unlike the drug czar Emma Littleport who floated about with ballerina grace, Ms. Cutter's plain black and white attire gave Daisy the impression that she might just waddle penguin-style across the platform.

"What you see with the naked eye is not always what's reality." Katharyn strode with confident steps as she nodded to the technician. The lights dimmed and PowerPoint filled the front screen. “Our eyes can fool us, even those trained to detect the minutest detail. Nobody gets every nuance perfectly. And that’s why our camera, whether still or video, is our closest collaborator.”

It seemed each woman who taught these lessons was just as knowledgeable as the next in their chosen field.

Katharyn continued, “Our cameras pick up the tiniest of objects and keep the scene intact even after it has been disassembled. What the forensic photographer does is capture a permanent record for the police officers but most importantly for the courts.”

A tiny hand was raised.

“Yes? Do you have a question or an observation?”

“An inquiry, actually,” The diminutive librarian, Miss Peabody, asked softly, as she nibbled on a fingernail and stood. “Before you begin, could you please tell us if you need a special degree for this line of work?” She sat, still chewing.

“Thank you. That’s a very good question. Of course it depends on the country where you apply. Here in the U.K., you must have at least 5 GCSEs and a degree in some scientific subject like biology.”

“Any special photography skills?” Another person asked. Was that the Converse- wearing kid? Daisy leaned forward. Yep, same torn-jeans and crew cut.

This time a small diamond glittered from his earlobe.

"No. But, of course, it's helpful if you know how to use one." Katharyn picked up a huge camera with a lens the size of a soup can. "And you must be able to work efficiently in chaotic and sometimes emotionally traumatic settings. It's not just using this equipment. You must have the personality to suit the job."

"Ta," the young man said.

"Shall I continue?"

Heads nodded.

Katharyn Cutter flicked to the next slide. "What do you think this is?"

"A metal object of some kind." A voice called from the rear.

"Maybe a kitchen knife?" Another person said from the front.

"How about a switchblade?"

The instructor zoomed the picture out and a swashbuckling sword filled the photo. She brought the real object out from behind the podium. "We can make magic with our lens but what we want is reality."

"Blimey."

"In this profession, you are required to preserve and protect the scene, determine what evidence is necessary, record, develop and capture fingerprint evidence in certain circumstances."

Daisy jotted the detailed list from the overhead slide into her notebook.

"Of utmost importance, you must never disturb evidence. It is paramount that the scene is kept orderly and intact."

Had Ms. Cutter done any of this at the lake where June had been found? Perhaps she was culpable in changing the crime scene to cover her tracks. Or had she taken the notes from the detective's desk? If so, why?

"We're going to take a test." Katharyn returned to the podium.

Moans circled the room.

Ms. Cutter smiled. "Everyone despises quizzes. But this will be fun, I guarantee it."

Daisy put aside her notebook. She loved tests and revered anything that challenged her mind. Who didn't want to keep their brains intact by exercising cells that made up one's intellect?

"These two pictures look exactly the same to the untrained eye but there are two things different in the second photo. Let's see who can discover what those two things are."

Murmurs. Two people rose and went to the front to look closer at the picture.

Daisy raised her hand. "There is a small knife in the right hand corner and a light on in the second picture that are not in the first."

"Well done." Ms. Cutter clapped. "That's the quickest I've ever had anyone discover those."

The two up front went back to their seats and several looked at Daisy and nodded approvals.

Allison patted Daisy's shoulder and beamed. A little affirmation went a long way in her world after how she had been treated by her fellow teachers all those years. A rain shower that saturated a dried sponge couldn't possibly be as affected as Daisy had been right then and there.

"So what did he say?" Allison prodded Daisy as they walked toward the break area when class was finished. "Did you discover anything new?"

"There's really nothing I can tell you."

"Of course there is. You must know something."

Jen, Val, and Fiona joined them in the hall.

"So?" Val asked. "Learn anything last night?"

"She's not saying," Allison said. "But she sure showed up the others in the class just now."

"Decker probably still thinks I had something to

do with June's death. And you know it, don't you Daisy?" Fiona pouted.

"I don't know any such thing." She held Fiona's elbow and walked beside her.

"Can you tell us whether it's—" Jen stopped. The others screeched to a halt as DS Decker approached.

Daisy was certain they must look like a group of mice that spotted the house cat.

"Good morning. I was just about to call everyone together into the conference area. Would you care to help me again?" He side-glanced in Daisy's direction and winked.

"Of course," Allison said. "We should each go back to the classes we just left and announce that they need to go to the main room right away."

"Great idea. Thank you." Decker continued down the hall.

"Caught the wink," Jen taunted and elbowed Daisy.

She blushed. "I don't know what you're talking about."

The group giggled as they parted, each back to where they had just come from.

Within minutes, the large conference area was abuzz with activity, loud chatter and chairs being shuffled.

Decker tapped on the microphone. "Can I please

have everyone's attention?"

As if God Himself spoke, the crowd ceased its pandemonium.

"I have an announcement I wish to make, and I want you to listen very carefully. I have managed to reach the police, and they should be with us within the next twenty-four hours."

The group heaved a gigantic sigh and some hugged their neighbors.

"It's been a long ordeal."

"But was it an accident?" Big Charles Bond shouted.

"We are examining further evidence."

"In other words, she was murdered." The man persisted and his wife nodded beside him.

"Right now we would prefer to wait before we announce our final conclusions. But thank you for asking." The detective diverted his attention from Big Charles. "What I would like you to do though is to be my pseudo partners. Those who attended my class know what I'm talking about."

Murmuring ensued and Daisy and Allison looked at each other. They'd been in his lecture. Plus Daisy also knew he was playing a game of manipulation with the crowd. Get them to participate, and they would be less likely to focus on the murderer if there was one.

"I've been remiss in my job." Decker riffled through his stack. "It seems I've misplaced some vital papers and I need your help."

Val, Jen, Allison and Fiona glanced at Daisy. Surely they guessed she already knew this information. Would they be angry that she hadn't told them and their trust in her chiseled away a tad?

"What I'm asking is that each of you become a sleuth at this precise moment. Look in every crevice, nook and corner. Leave no stone unturned. Once again, I ask you to form your groups of ten and enter the areas where you were before. I will come in each room and delegate a portion of the conference center to you. It will be your responsibility to scour every inch of this place. I need those files." Decker stepped down and the crowd dispersed into separate quarters.

"You knew, didn't you?" Fiona asked.

"He asked me not to say anything."

Fiona issued a *humph* and tromped away.

Allison stepped up to Daisy. "I understand that you couldn't divulge that. And Fi will forgive you, too. Just give her a few minutes. Okay?"

The ladies disappeared into the crowd and headed to their assigned place. For a moment, Daisy was alone in the midst of the moving horde.

CHAPTER 16

"I'm sorry I got angry." Fiona walked beside Daisy. The other three ladies followed as they left the main conference room.

"It's okay. I understand."

"You can't possibly understand. Decker's *convinced* I've murdered June."

"But I don't believe it."

"I know, and that's why I shouldn't be upset with you. I'm sorry."

"He'll figure this out. I'm sure of it."

As they stepped outside, the barbaric, bitter wind pierced Daisy's face and the exposed skin on her wrists. She lowered her head and shielded her eyes to avoid the worst of it.

Mother Nature was obviously upset with the

murderous injustice done in this place and was making her feelings known to everyone.

From the distance, a low mist hung atop the lake where only a day before Daisy had found the pink hat and the body of June Fellows.

The eerie haze over the water was something akin to a clip from the Sleepy Hollow series. Ichabod Crane had to solve a mystery, but his crime involved the infamous headless horseman. Daisy shuddered at the thought. She wasn't easily spooked but was certain she'd stay well clear of the lake the next time she returned to this normally beautiful setting.

Daisy and the others followed the housekeeper, whose keys jangled from her gloved hand, into Waterside foyer. They disrobed heavy coats and scarfs and hung them on hooks inside the door, and waited a few minutes to adjust to the extremes in temperature from outside to in.

"Let's go into each bedroom on one side and then come up the other." Allison wiped moisture from her glasses and replaced them back on her face.

"It's going to feel strange going into other people's rooms. I wouldn't want someone I didn't know rifling through my things," Fiona said.

"Everyone's agreed to allow us to check under beds and mattresses for the lost paperwork as long as we stay out of personal belongings. We need to find out who's responsible for harming June."

How to locate something with such slim parameters seemed impossible to Daisy. But they agreed to keep their sleuthing to the designated areas with the housekeeper as their guide.

"Besides, this is a crowd of crime writers. They want to solve the misdeed that's been done. My guess is several folks are already making notes about our situation and will someday write bestsellers about it. Purely fiction, mind you." Jen's rosy cheeks glowed coal red as she rubbed fingertips over them.

"I still wouldn't want someone going into my space."

Val sat in an entry lounge chair and rearranged the socks in her boots. She looked up, and her brows sloped downward. "How else would we find what Decker lost if we couldn't go into these rooms?"

"I'm not thoroughly convinced he's lost anything. This could just be a wild goose chase." Fiona pounded her wet feet and motioned the rest to follow the housekeeper who was now on the move.

"Why would he do that?" Daisy asked, as she walked behind Fiona.

"To keep everyone occupied."

"It seems to be working," Allison said.

"But what a waste of time if there really isn't anything missing."

"We need to trust Decker. He's doing what he deems best." Daisy's overprotective nature toward this rather unknown man surprised even her.

"Should we begin on the right or left?" Val asked.

"Let's begin numerically. That's this one on the right." Allison stepped up and the housekeeper unlocked the first room.

"AFTER TWO HOURS of upturning mattresses and scouring rooms, we're still empty-handed." Fiona closed the third-floor door at the end of the hallway. "I don't want to look under another mattress the rest of my life."

"Me either. Let's go and get some cocoa or tea," Daisy led the way to the stairwell. "We need to retrieve our coats and scarfs. Hopefully they've dried out by now."

At the bottom of the stairs, Fiona pushed the fire exit door that opened into the foyer. With a shove, she accidently hit Katharyn Cutter in the shoulder, and Emma Littleport trailed behind her.

"I'm sorry." Fiona stepped back from the incoming duo.

"Never mind. We're fine." Katharyn and Emma rushed up the stairs, shoving Val, Jen, Allison and Daisy out of the way as if a mad dog were in pursuit.

"How rude," Fiona said, as she watched them ascend the steps two at a time.

"What do you suppose that's all about?" Allison exited as Fiona held the door.

"Not sure. But they sure seemed in a hurry."

"They acted like they didn't even see us."

"I wonder if something's going on that we don't know about?" Val followed the others into the foyer.

"I don't know what's up with them, but I'm ready for that cup of tea. How about you, ladies?" Val asked.

"Maybe we'll learn some news when we get back." Daisy slipped on her coat. The sticky note with a phone number scribbled on it fell out of her pocket. She'd found the note right there in the lobby after discovering the body and everyone had dispersed. "Do any of you know whose number this might be? 07717850351?"

"No. And I'd suggest you ring it, but the phones still don't work," Jen said.

"Then how did Decker know the police would be here within twenty-four hours?"

Fiona shoved her arms in her coat sleeves as if wrestling with them. "Now that's a good question.

Was the detective lying? And if so, was he lying about the losing something? Told you he couldn't be trusted."

"There does seem to be inconsistencies with what he says." Allison's puzzled look swept over the other women's faces.

"Come on, ladies. Let's not draw any conclusions." Daisy played advocate once more as she pulled on a glove.

"I hope you aren't disappointed with your knight in shining armor. Who knows? Maybe Decker had something to do with June's death. We automatically trust him because he's a policemen, but should we?" Fiona asked.

"Of course we should. He's done nothing to warrant suspicion. In fact, he's handled this situation quite remarkably."

"And you are one of the nicest, most naïve people I know, Daisy."

"I like to give people the benefit of the doubt." She shrugged. "What's wrong with that?"

"Nothing. But seems to me you should be more careful in who you trust. I don't want to see you get hurt."

"Believe me, I've no plans to allow that to happen." Daisy pulled open the door and led the group out of Waterside. "Watch your steps, ladies. This little slope to the sidewalk tends to be slippery with this crushed snow. Luckily, I'm fairly sure-footed having grown up in— Whoa!"

Sliding forward, right heel leading the way, her arms flailed as she grasped for something to lay hold of.

Daisy's knuckles struck something as she tried to regain her footing.

"Ouch!"

Jen and Fiona came on either side of Daisy, slid their hands under her armpits, and steadied her upright.

"Thank you, ladies. I thought I was going down for sure. And at my age, something was bound to break. Allison? Where's—" Daisy looked over her shoulder. "Oh, no."

Allison held a gloved hand over her left eye, and a grimace of pain contorted her mouth. Her glasses sat on the path with a lopsided earpiece and one broken lens.

Daisy reached for the spectacles, straightened the twisted piece and gave them to her friend. "I'm so sorry. I didn't mean to knock these off when I slipped."

"It's no problem. Honestly. I go through several

pairs a month." She smiled and groaned. "I'm fine. Really."

"I'll pay to have them repaired."

"It was an accident."

"I insist."

"Thank you. I appreciate the offer, and we can work out the details later."

Daisy patted Jen and Fiona's arms. "Thank you both so much. I could have broken something besides Allison's glasses."

"You're welcome. That's what friends are for. Saving us from ourselves."

"Maybe that's what you are trying to do with Decker, too, huh? Trying to save me from myself?" Daisy brushed dampness off her trousers and bottom.

Fiona draped an arm around Daisy's shoulders. "We're here for each other. If he does anything to hurt you, he'll have to answer to me."

"And me." Jen linked arms with Daisy on the other side.

"Me too." Val grabbed Jen's hand.

"Count me in." Allison put her misshapen specs on, came alongside and linked arms with Fiona. A human chain of friendship.

The warm library was filled with coat-laden

attendees who faced the far side of the room. Decker stood on a chair and waved a manila folder. “Ladies and gentlemen, we’ve found the missing papers.”

Fiona elbowed Daisy. “I told you he had it all along.”

CHAPTER 17

"How convenient." Daisy offered a cold, accusatory tone as she approached Decker. The crowd seemed to fade into the woodwork and they were alone on an island. And not an idyllic one with swaying palm trees. But one surrounded by piranhas swimming close to the shore.

"What do you mean?" His big brown eyes swelled with surprise as he stepped off the chair.

"Seems you found your folder after you sent everyone on a wild goose chase."

"What makes you think it was a wild chase?"

"Where did you discover it, then?" Daisy managed to lower her tone to a pitch below hysterical and the others around them slowly came back into view. The smell of tea steeping and windows coated with moisture were reality, but this conversation drenched with suspicion seemed unreal.

Decker placed a warm hand on her shoulder. "Believe it or not they were found in the pre-fabricated lab we set up for the crime scene class. I wasn't sending everyone hither and yon for no reason."

A tingling sensation traveled down her elbow and wrist at his touch. She wiggled her fingertips, swallowed and whispered, "Where was the lab set up?"

"Remember the yellow tape and white coat I had as props in the classroom?" Decker released her shoulder. "Behind that was a makeshift lab but it'd been draped with a large cloth. We were going to use it later in the week for some hands-on training."

"Who'd have known that equipment was there?"

"Only the teachers as far as I know. Charles Bond and his wife stumbled on it when they were rummaging around."

Daisy cocked her head. "Why were they in there? Maybe they have something to do with this."

"It was their assigned area to look."

"I see. So you're thinking it's purely the teachers who are complicit in hiding the folder?"

"It appears so. I've had my suspicions, but I haven't been able to put my finger on any reason they'd want to hurt that woman."

"But which ones are involved?"

"I'm going to find out soon enough. Now that I have these." He fanned the sheaf of papers in the air.

"Oh, no you don't." William Shanks seemed to come from nowhere, zipped up to the detective and ripped the folder from his hands.

"Stop that man!" DS Decker shouted.

Before anyone could grab William Shanks, he was gone.

The DS rushed to the center of the room and directed several men to follow the elusive Shanks. "Go after him. He's obviously implicated somehow in those documents. But he won't get far."

"HOW IS it you couldn't find him?" Decker spoke to the group of men who returned empty handed. "There aren't too many places to hide in this god-forsaken place."

"Not sure, sir."

"Where are Katharyn and Emma? Barbara Bloom? I need to speak to those ladies as well."

"They seemed to have left."

"That's not possible. The roads are impassable. Otherwise the police would've been here by now."

"We saw the women running up the stairs as we

were heading here. Like someone had screamed 'fire,' and they were rushing to put it out," Daisy said.

"We'll keep looking for them and Shanks." Charles Bond made his way to the front of the men. "I promise you, none of them will get away if I can help it."

"What is it that you do?" The detective held the large man's forearm. "You seem to have a lot to say, even when not asked."

Big Charles's wife joined him. "We work for the same publication as June Fellows, who by the way was actually Janet Commons. She used an alias and claimed she was a student."

Decker released Charles. "And what was she trying to uncover? Why didn't I know anything about this?"

"June, I mean, *Jane* had begun to confide in us just before we came to this conference."

"Why are you telling me now?"

"Because she didn't get the chance to fill us in on names and details. Just said that individuals attending this week were under suspicion for serious criminal activity." Big Charles stood toe to toe with Decker.

"We decided to come and keep an eye on her." Mrs. Bond laid a hand on her husband's arm and he stepped back from the detective.

"You fools! Obviously you didn't do a very good job. Now she's dead and that Shanks fellow has some of the incriminating evidence."

Charles and his wife bowed their heads.

"You will answer to me later. After we get out of here and out of this mess."

Steam rose higher on the windows and the confined space caused a drum to beat in Daisy's temples. She rubbed them in small circles to release the stress. "We need to find out what June was after and who's responsible."

"Are you all right?" Allison shuffled through the crowd and guided Daisy by the arm. "You look like you're going to faint. Maybe you should go outside and get some fresh air."

"Thank you. I'll be fine."

"We agree." Jen, Val and Fiona encompassed Daisy and gave a circle of protection as they escorted her toward the door.

Daisy did an about-face. "Seems like you're back to square one, detective."

"That's not exactly true."

"What do you mean?"

"Shanks took one folder, but I had another one already in my desk locked up. He probably had no idea there were two."

Daisy advanced toward him and away from the

ladies. "Why don't you read it here and now? See who else is involved."

"I want to review it on my own, and I'm going to do that right this minute."

"Is Fiona still a suspect?" She looked back at her friend.

"I've no idea. Not yet anyway. So I expect—" Decker looked away from Daisy and addressed the crowd. "I expect that no one will leave until I've had a chance to review those papers."

"But Daisy needs to go outside for a few minutes."

"That includes everyone." Decker glanced at her. "Everyone." He spun around and walked away.

"Why that foolish man." Fiona followed after him. "I'll give him a piece of my mind."

Daisy grabbed Fiona. "You'll do no such thing. You're already on his bad side. Don't make things worse."

"But you need some fresh air."

"How about some cool water instead?" Allison, conjured up a full cup of water, handed her the glass.

Daisy sipped a few drops and the drumming in her temples stopped.

"What are we suppose to do now?" Jen's smooth skin beaded with sweat along her forehead. "It's like a sauna in here."

"Let's open the windows a bit and let some air in. It won't take long to cool the place off," Val said.

Each woman opened a window slightly but wide enough to let Mister Frost sweep in with enough gusto to drop the temperature a centigrade.

"Listen," Val shouted. The whirr of conversation halted.

"What's wrong?" Jen asked.

"You hear that?"

"No."

"Exactly. The clang of the radiators has stopped. The heaters have shut off."

They slammed the windows simultaneously.

"We could freeze in here if it stays off too long."

The last hiss of air from the radiator nearby assured Daisy that within a short amount of time the temperature in the building would drop to uncomfortably dangerous levels.

CHAPTER 18

"Get some candles and matches." Daisy remained calm. She mentally reached back to a teaching year when she helped direct a group of children during an unexpected and particularly violent thunderstorm. That moment had taught her the fine art of cool pretension.

"Torches are in here." A member of the cooking staff pulled open a deep drawer and handed out flashlights. Daisy always imagined cavemen with massive flames on sticks when she heard the word torch.

"We need to keep the doors and windows shut. Hold what warmth that's left in here."

"Maybe it's only in this part of the building. Let me check and see if it's still on where the kettles are plugged in." Allison shifted to the far side of the area by the tea supplies. "There doesn't seem to be any electricity here either."

"What are we going to do?" screeched the librarian from a corner.

"Not panic." Daisy wrapped her arms around Miss Peabody and squeezed.

"But how will we stay warm?"

"We'll make do. If need be, we'll have the staff bring blankets from the linen storage."

Daisy had seen this panic before, on the faces of the scared children during the thunderstorm. She could practically feel fear slither in and take charge over the crowd. Something had to be done to stop it before chaos erupted.

"Wait! I know." Daisy released the librarian. "Let's sing. That always makes everyone calm down and feel better."

"Sing? At a time like this?" A shiver seemed to make Miss' Peabody shake more. She perched on the arm of a nearby chair and held tightly.

"Of course. Like you might have done on school trips." Daisy nodded toward her and smiled.

"What song do you suggest?" Val asked.

"How about *Green and Pleasant Land*?"

"Actually it's called *Jerusalem*. But that doesn't seem—"

"Why not? I rather like it and I'm not even

British. Its England's unofficial national anthem, like "God Bless America" is for the United States, isn't it?"

"Yes. I've heard that but I don't take much stock in it."

"Who knows what year that song was first sung?" Daisy asked, determined to keep the nervous group of adults from succumbing to anxiety. Panic wouldn't serve anyone any good.

"I know." Miss Peabody rose on unsteady legs. "It was first performed in 1916 during WW I at a patriotic 'Fight for Right' concert at Queens' Hall in London." She sat on the chair this time with her legs curled under and hugging her chest. "But there isn't any green and pleasantness in what we're going through right now."

"That's okay. We can pretend it's green. Can someone get us started with the lyrics?"

A deep, tenor voice pierced the semi-darkness and began to sing, "And did those feet in ancient times..."

Men removed their hats, held them to their sides and joined in. Women added their voices to the growing music. The acoustics were perfect, as if they were singing in a professional amphitheater. Only an organ or piano accompaniment was missing. But, to Daisy's relief, the miraculous a cappella was enough to chase the fear monster away with each stanza.

DS Decker stepped into the room. Apparently, he'd finished reading the folders, but he waited until the choir finished belting out the song before he spoke. "I have some news."

Instant quiet came over the library except for hissing from the flickering candles.

"IT WAS GREED. June Fellows was trying to expose an illegal operation."

"Are you absolutely sure?" In spite of the cold that penetrated Daisy's coat and gloves, a bead of sweat made its way along the nape of her neck. Terror had reappeared and now held her hostage.

"It's in here." The detective slapped the pages with a flat palm.

"What did she find out that warranted someone drowning her in the lake?"

"June Fellows, a.k.a. Jane Commons, wasn't drowned. She was strangled, then taken to the lake in the hopes her body wouldn't be discovered until the culprits were long gone." Decker faced Daisy. "Only you happened to go out that morning and foiled their plans."

"Why would anyone do such a thing?"

"To make millions to begin with. Money bewitches people into acting crazy."

Big Charles puffed out his chest and wrapped an arm around his wife's waist. "I remember the case in 2011 when the dismissal of 160 police officers for offences ranging from assault to leaking confidential information was hushed up. There's always someone willing to sell their soul."

"In this case, I believe they were fed up with the way our country's leadership was heading and wanted to make a point." Decker addressed the crowd.

"What point?" Jen drew near Daisy.

"That people should make their own destinies, not governments." The detective placed the papers under his arm and rubbed his hands together.

"But when one or two take charge, disorder reigns. We might not agree on every decision our leaders make, but we need to stay united in the final decisions, otherwise democracy fails." Allison walked a few steps and sidled next to Jen.

"There are a few loose ends, though. Whatever's in the notes Mr. Swank has will help unravel the rest of this puzzle. It appears there were at least one, if not two, people involved as masterminds behind the selling of the secrets and Ms. Commons murder.

There had to be. But there was no mention of names in this folder, just hints that could link others."

"You mean there's still a murderer in our midst?" Miss Peabody sneezed and continued to shiver in the chair.

"Yes. So we must continue to be vigilant."

"But what about Shanks and the others, Emma and Katharyn? What about Barbara Bloom. Where's she? Was she involved?" Questions rang out like bullets without giving the detective a chance to reply.

Daisy raised a hand, and Decker nodded toward her. "How about my friend, Fiona?"

"Seems her name was only mentioned because June thought she might be getting close to finding out what she was up to."

"How would I have done that?" Fiona locked arms with Daisy.

"I guess during the Play to Stage competition she dropped her briefcase and papers fell out. She made a note on the margin that you were standing next to her and made a face. She was certain you'd read something incriminating."

"The only face I was making was being ticked-off. She stole my part, and I wanted revenge. I didn't see anything except red."

"So you're exonerated, Fiona." Daisy squeezed her.

Val, Jen and Allison hugged the two of them and created a circle. The Stonehenge groupies were united and their friend was now free from any suspicion.

Daisy and the others let go and Fiona sighed. "What a relief."

"But there's still the problem of who was behind the whole scheme," Daisy said.

"Yes. You're right," Decker added. "We need to get those papers from Shanks and wrap up this case once and for all."

CHAPTER 19

Daisy was certain the library was closing in on her. Try as she might to stay composed, the gnawing beast of apprehension nibbled at her mind. With the library totally dark, except the candles that now burned low, imaginary creatures lurked in every corner. She loved books, but the bindings along the shelves held fiendish images.

"How long will this go on?" Fiona asked no one in particular, her voice tense.

"I'm not sure." Daisy's teeth chattered, and she put a gloved hand over her mouth and jaw.

Decker took charge. He accompanied a staff member to the linen closet, brought back a stack of heavy duvets and handed them out. The crowd sat around the perimeter and shared the covers. "Let's take turns guarding the room so that others can get rest. I'll be first. Charles you can stand guard with me." He pointed to two gentlemen, a younger man with blond spikes, the other a gray-haired man with a slight osteoporosis-arched back. "Then you and you can take the next shift."

Daisy sat on the floor next to Fiona, pulled her knees up and drew the blanket tighter.

"When will we be able to go and find those imbeciles?" The Converse-wearing kid had been quiet up until now but seemed ready to take on the potential killers. Everyone appeared edgy and Daisy was sure it would take a miracle for Decker to maintain calm in the midst of this rumbling tempest—inside and out.

"We'll have to wait until morning to do any more searches." Decker wrapped a blanket around his shoulders, pulled a chair by the door and sat.

"But they could get a long way from here in the meantime." Converse got up and flexed his scrawny muscles beneath his jacket.

Decker patted the air and the lad sat back down.

"Like I said, I don't think they're going anywhere. We need to stay calm. And remember we have the dining hall with the food right here. They'll be looking to eat sooner or later."

"Speaking of food, we could make sandwiches

and pass those around before we try to sleep." Daisy stood. Maybe moving would shake off her jitters.

"Great idea. Let me help." Allison jumped up and clapped her arms a few times to warm herself, then strode next to Daisy into the kitchen.

"Okay ladies, we need an assembly line behind the silver countertop," Allison directed. "Val and Jen, please lay out single slices of bread on a tray. Fiona, will you swipe each piece with butter and then move the tray down to me. I'll put cheese on and Daisy can add pieces of ham."

Like Rosie the Riveter, the women rolled up their proverbial sleeves and took charge of feeding the crowd. A bit like Jesus provided for the five thousand. Although their numbers weren't as big as His, it seemed a miracle would be helpful to get through the night right about now.

Mrs. Bond, Charles's wife stacked the finished sandwiches into piles and handed them out to those seated on the floor.

"Not only are they going to want food, they'll want warmth and eventually need water." Decker joined the women in the kitchen. "Thanks for suggesting this, Daisy."

In the darkened room, she felt the burn on her face. The day might never come she could take a compliment and not be embarrassed, but she was eternally grateful for the opportunity to try.

Decker turned and once again addressed the crowd, "Plus everyone will want to take a shower once the electricity comes back on. There are plenty of daily necessities our criminals will be after, and that's when we'll nab them."

"How do you know they won't leave the grounds? If they get their cars started they might try."

"It was indicated on the registration form how people were getting to the conference, and I reviewed the list earlier. The only one who came by an automobile was Emma, and I believe her husband dropped her off. I had the lab equipment with me, so of course I have my vehicle. Otherwise, everyone else rode the train."

"So those crooks must be here somewhere?"

Decker nodded. "And now that we've had something to eat, let's attempt to get some sleep. It's going to be a long night regardless, so the least we can do is try our best to rest."

"We'll clean up the kitchen and then get under the duvets." Allison's servant heart was never more evident than when she helped in a crisis. "It will only take a few minutes."

The comfort of work to be done and clatter of

dishes piled into the deep kitchen basins was exactly what Daisy needed to make the apprehension go dormant.

Once finished, the ladies returned to their places and cuddled under the warmth of the covers.

Daisy shifted sideways and closed her eyes.

Creak. Creak.

She jolted from semi-consciousness. That split second between dreams and reality. "Who's there?" She whispered.

"Shhh. It's only me." Decker sat beside her. "Someone's left this area but didn't leave the building. Charles and I were stationed at both exits."

"Who's gone?"

"Allison."

Daisy sat upright. "Has something happened to her?" Panic replaced the small amount of peace that she'd felt while cleaning up.

"She's not in her spot. I used the torch to check on each person. Did a headcount."

"Maybe she's just gone to the ladies room." Daisy rubbed her eyes and the woolen gloves only made the stinging persist. She was allergic to down feathers but there was no way she would say anything. She was grateful for the warmth.

Creak. Creak.

Decker put a forefinger to his lips.

The aged floorboards crunched under the smallest amount of weight.

Daisy inhaled. Waited.

Creak.

She couldn't take the suspense any longer, flung her blanket away and sprang off the floor. "Who's there?"

"Gosh, Daisy it's only me." Allison's crooked glasses reflected the last flick of candlelight from the sideboard. "Why are you yelling at me?" She choked on her words.

"Where were you?" The detective demanded.

"I was...was...only going to finish putting the dishes in the machine so there'd be less work in the morning."

"Foolish woman! Are you trying to frighten everyone with your tiptoeing around? We thought you were someone trying to get in." Decker pushed out an exasperated breath.

Allison whimpered. "I was only trying to help."

"It's okay." Daisy took her by the arm and drew her to the floor. "But we should really stay together. What if someone wicked had been in the kitchen?"

Gasp. "Do you really think someone could be in here?" Allison's eyes fluttered back and forth with fright.

Daisy patted her. "It's all right. We're together

now and you're safe. DS Decker won't let anything happen to us. Will you?"

"Ma'am, I'm doing the best I know how under the circumstances but, no one, and I mean no one leaves." He directed his threat to Allison, "Do I make myself clear?"

"Yes, sir. I understand."

"Right. Now everyone listen to me. We have at least three potential convicts in the vicinity. And two professional felons. Please do not leave this area without first telling me."

Nods shadowed the walls.

"We don't want another death on our hands. What I'm asking is for you to rest and let us take our rounds of keeping an eye on all of you. Are you ready, Charles?"

"Yes, sir." The large man buttoned his coat.

Daisy put an arm around Allison who quickly relaxed, let out a small puff of air and snored softly on Daisy's shoulder.

CHAPTER 20

Daisy shifted positions as her legs throbbed and her mind played tricks at every squeak, shuffle, or movement made by others. The hours of darkness were long, drawn out minutes that tortuously ticked along.

"Psst. Are you awake?" Allison stirred next to her.

"I never went to sleep."

"What a shame. I'm afraid I can sleep just about anywhere when I'm knackered." Allison yawned with a quiet stretch. "What time is it anyway?"

Daisy tapped the light on her watch. "Five-thirty."

"It won't be daylight for another three hours. Guess I'll go back to sleep." With that Allison rolled over, reeled the blanket in and released a muffled snore.

Daisy got up and went to the window. The snow had stopped falling and the full moon, puffed with white wonder paid no attention to the earthly inhabitants shivering below. It slipped beneath thick clouds, and Daisy held her breath waiting for the guardian of the skies to reappear.

"Are you all right?

Daisy leapt.

"I'm sorry I didn't mean to startle you." Decker's shoulder brushed hers with a light stroke, and proved that electricity could spark even without the help of turbines and power stations. Who would have guessed a nuclear reaction could occur by the simple touching of two human bodies in close enough proximity.

Daisy nodded toward the seated, blond-spiked young man who cleaned under his nails with a pen tip. "I thought you were taking a break and the other two were on guard."

"I was supposed to."

"You couldn't sleep either, I guess."

He shrugged. "It's hard when my mind's swirling with a thousand thoughts. I'm gutted by what's happened, and there are so many things I should've done differently. That I wished hadn't occurred."

Daisy looked into his dark eyes, a deep well of intense emotion. "We all feel that way sometimes."

"But I shouldn't have allowed it."

A door handle rattled and the spiked lad jumped from his chair. "Sir, sir, someone's trying to get in." He beckoned to Decker who rushed over.

Daisy put a hand to the base of her neck. Blood vessels hammered with a vengeance, and she inhaled and exhaled deeply to stem the pulsing throb.

DS Decker pulled the door open with a jerk.

William Shanks spilled onto the floor with the blue lips and bulging eyes of a madman. "I ne…ee… ed…" Shanks fainted at the detective's feet.

Decker pulled him up by the coat collar and shook. "Where are the others and what did you do with the folder?"

"I don't know. Honestly." William withered in the detective's grasp.

"But you took the thing, so what did you do with it?"

"They offered to pay me if I could get my hands on it."

"Who did?"

"That ice-queen Emma, and her nasty sidekicks Cutter and Bloom."

"Did you give the papers to them?" Decker released his lapel with a shove and Shanks landed on the chair the spiked lad had vacated.

"Yes."

"You scoundrel." The detective raised a flat palm toward him.

Shanks curled his arms over his head. "Stop. I didn't mean to do anything wrong. I thought if I got the folder and was able to read it before I gave it to them, I could figure out who else was involved with June's death. Then they shoved me into a closet and locked me in."

"Did you get a chance to read it?"

Shanks's eyes flitted. The crazed look totally overtook his handsome features. "I'm not saying."

Decker lifted him from the chair by his coat's shoulders. "You better say. Now!"

"No way. I want to stay alive. If I snitch, I'm a dead man."

"You're a dead man anyway." Decker dragged him to the back room where earlier he'd read his other notes. Cups on the teacart rattled as he slammed the door.

"What do you suppose he's going to do to him?" Fiona asked, buttoning her coat.

"I've no idea." Daisy scrutinized the door where Decker and Swanks had gone. The detective was exhausted, and when fatigue attacked the sense of perspective was lost. She'd been there plenty of times.

Hiss. Gurgle. Hiss. Pop.

"The radiators are warming up," Jen squealed.

"Which means we might have electricity, too." Val flicked the wall switch on.

Sconces along the paneled walls lit up with a bright glow.

Daisy joined the others in jumping up and down. With the heavy coats and hats, it looked more like a polar bear aerobics class than a group of worn and weary prisoners.

"What should we do? Can we go back to our bedrooms and shower?" Allison gathered the blanket and draped it around her shoulders. "Hot water should be coming up promptly."

"How about some food? Surely I'm not the only one peckish?" Jen's youthful glow matched the light from the sconce.

"Let's gather the staff and have them get the kitchen going again. But I don't believe we should leave the building yet. Until we speak with Decker at least."

"I want to go to my room." Fiona gave a small stomp.

"Me too. If we go in groups, we'd be safe, right?" Val went to Fiona as a defense partner.

"Look what they did to Shanks, locking him up and frightening him half to death."

Big Charles pounded his fist into the palm of his

hand. "I'm not going to let that happen to me. I say we leave in groups of four or five to be sure."

"Nobody's going anywhere. Not until I say so." His wife moved from the shadows and held the long saber that had been used as a prop in Katharyn's photography class.

"What in the world are you doing?" Charles' cheeks swelled in anger as he reached out to grab her arm.

"Shut up, you Scouser." Mrs. Bond jiggled the sword.

"But, honey?" He backed into the woodwork.

"Don't honey me. I'm tired of your loud-mouthed, obnoxious behavior. You're an embarrassment to me and the children."

"But?"

"I said, be quiet." His wife moved toward the throng, swinging the sword with short waves as they backed away. "And that means each of you."

Daisy took a baby step toward her, hands up in surrender. "You don't have to harm anyone. I'm sure you didn't mean to do anything to June."

"What are you talking about?"

"You killed June Fellows, didn't you?" Daisy inched further toward her.

"I did no such thing."

"Then why are you wielding that thing and threatening everyone."

"Because you're a bunch of eejits."

"Did you have anything to do with William taking the folder and helping out Emma and Katharyn?"

Charles whispered, "My wife needs her meds. She gets like this sometimes."

His wife swung around. "Seriously? *I* need medication? The only reason I need anything is to numb me from living with you all these years. I finally found purpose and it has nothing to do with you."

"What do you mean?"

"If you say another word, I'm going to slice that tongue off of yours."

Big Charles clamped his mouth closed and his lips formed a thin line of pain.

Mrs. Bond raised the sword overhead.

CHAPTER 21

Daisy ducked as Big Charles' wife circled the sword overhead with another wide sweep.

Groups of three and four huddled together and gasps ricocheted the walls.

"NO! She's going to kill someone." A middle-aged woman, with perfectly manicured nails and wearing an emerald-green pantsuit, clutched her chest and started to crumple as if her knees had dissolved into jelly. A gentleman nearby gently guided her to a chair.

Decker appeared from nowhere, came up behind Mrs. Bond and grabbed her wrist. "It's not nice to play with sharp objects."

"Let go," she yelled.

"I'll keep squeezing until you drop the sword." The detective held fast and gave her arm a shake.

"Ouch!" She released the sword and it seemed to descend in slow motion and hit the floor with a deafening clang. "Let. Me. Go."

The detective pulled her hands behind her back. "I'll free you if you promise not to run."

She nodded and rubbed her wrist when Decker set her free.

"What in the world did you think you were doing?" Decker picked up the weapon. "You could've seriously injured someone. And where did you get this thing?"

"I took it when we were looking around for the folder. I thought it might come in handy. And I was right."

"What are you talking about?"

"These fools were trying to leave with those killers roaming out there. I was just trying to protect them."

"Ya got a funny way of showing protection, lady." The Converse lad ran fingers through his hair and exhaled a low whistle.

"I'm sure we can sort this out. Everyone just needs to calm down," Decker said.

"So you didn't have anything to do with the crime?" Allison heaved a loud sigh of relief.

"Of course not."

Big Charles came alongside his spouse. "I told you she sometimes gets this way, especially when she's frightened."

She melted into his arms and burst into tears. "What have I done? Oh, dear, me. What have I done?"

"It's all right." He cradled her and rubbed her hair gently as if she were an infant. "It's all right." Beauty and the beast retreated to a dark corner.

Decker's presence had brought reassurance to the crowd, and anxiety over the wielding swashbuckler dissolved. He nodded toward the window. ""Let's have breakfast everyone. Now that the weather seems to be clearing, we can go on a manhunt for the other two once we've had something to eat."

Daisy approached the detective by the window. Icicles hanging along the roofline began to slowly melt under the warming sun. Large water droplets plopped on the sidewalks and created miniature pools. "Did Shanks tell you anything?"

"He collapsed the minute I got him in the room. Try as I might, I couldn't get a peep from him."

"So you're no further than before?"

"It appears so, but I can't help but wonder if I'm missing something here."

"Like what?"

"I'm not sure."

"I was convinced Mrs. Bond had something to do with it." Daisy tilted her head toward the cowering couple.

"So did I, when I first came out and saw her with this thing." He raised the sword to waist height. "But I could tell, even with coming up from the rear, that she was acting more like a cornered animal than an assassin. I've seen too many like her not to recognize the symptoms."

Daisy shuddered. "You said in class that people can find a variety of ways to wound others. They don't need a gun. How silly of Katharyn to bring that sword here. But then again we're talking about someone who's a potential murderer."

"I'm going to put this in a safe place, then I'll join you and the others in the dining room." Decker's brown eyes were no longer shadowed with intense vexation as they'd been earlier when he grabbed William. Instead, calmness settled in those deep wells of his, and the tension in his facial muscles relaxed.

Bacon and egg aromas filtered into the library, and the meal bell elicited cheers from the crowd. The throng rushed to the cafeteria and fell into queue along the buffet's assembly line.

Rattle of dishes and nattering at the table almost made Daisy believe that June had never been killed and last night was just a horrible nightmare. But she wasn't that gullible to imagine there wasn't still danger in those teachers and perhaps even others sitting around her eating toast and beans.

DAISY LEANED back in the chair, licked her sticky lips of the last vestiges of syrup from the stack of pancakes and followed the wonderful taste with a long swig of hot coffee. "I needed that."

"We all did." Allison cleared the plates and set them on the end of the table to be collected by the staff.

"I can't believe we're still captive in this place. But the food satiated any need to rush back to our bedrooms." Fiona sipped her tea then handed the empty mug to Allison.

"I can't wait for a hot shower," Jen said.

"I'm a bath person myself." Val took her time eating the last of the eggs on her plate. The golden yolk smear left what appeared to be a wide smile.

"I don't care what kind of wash I have, but I need to do something with this hair."

To Daisy, the friendly conversation was reminiscent of morning coffee around the office break room. Her teaching years were over, and she was glad of it. Otherwise she would've never had the privilege of meeting such special people here in Branick.

She closed her eyes. Surrounds sounds of kitchen cleanup and the low-buzz of chitchat slowed her heart to a steady beat of thank-you, thank-you, thank-you. They'd made it through the night, and they would survive whatever came next.

"Tired?" Decker sat down next to her.

She opened her eyes. "Not really. Just relaxing."

"I'm glad you're able to unwind a bit. It's been a stressful time for everyone."

"It's still a bit chilly in here though." Daisy pulled up the coat she'd draped on the chair, and the detective helped with gentlemanly gesture of aiding her arm into a sleeve. As she shrugged the coat on, the yellow sticky note in her pocket floated gracefully like an autumnal leaf to the floor.

"You dropped this." He leaned over and picked it up.

"I keep forgetting about it. I found it under the chair in the Waterside foyer right after everyone dispersed to take care of June's body. But I've no idea whose number it is."

Decker pulled his mobile out of his pocket. "With

the storm over, it looks like we have reception again. Want me to ring it?"

"Sure."

He tapped the digits into his mobile and waited.

A phone jangled. Talking in the room stopped, and heads turned toward the noise of the chime.

Daisy's mouth dropped open. *No, it couldn't be.* Of all people, she never would have suspected... "It's *you*?

CHAPTER 22

Daisy nearly fell out of her chair as Decker jumped from his seat. His chair tottered and hit the floor with a *whump*. "You?"

Everyone in the dining area sat perfectly still and resembled mannequins in a front window.

The petite librarian, Miss Peabody, nudged her oversized glasses up onto her turned-up nose with a forefinger, and rose with a Napoleonic stance—her hand jammed into her suit jacket, chest puffed and head held high. She barked, "What do you *think* I've done?"

"You know exactly what you've done. Your number was found in the foyer the morning of June's death." Decker waved the sticky note.

"Finding my number doesn't mean a thing."

"Can you explain why it was there?"

Daisy stood beside Decker. "You've been playing the frightened puppy extremely well." She clapped three times in mock approval. "You should be awarded an Emmy for your performance."

"I've no idea what you're talking about."

"You whined and sniveled at every turn. You fooled me into comforting you." Daisy had never truly appreciated the theory that when anger went unchecked you saw red, until this very moment. Her temples pulsed and hands sweat with the urge to harm someone. Those years of pent-up fury with her coworkers' attitude now exploded. "I loathe. Being. Used."

The librarian smirked. "But you're so gullible. So naïve."

Decker put an arm around Daisy's shoulder and squeezed. "Don't let her get to you. She's not worth losing your temper or self-respect. You're much better than that."

Time stopped. In that split second, the slight pressure of his touch liberated the long-held anger in Daisy's soul. Decker's confidence in her character spoke volumes and pumped her self-worth into blimp-sized proportion. Never again would she allow others to dictate her emotions or reactions.

That part of her life was over. She was free. "Thank you."

The detective released Daisy and smiled. "I've met too many like her. You could go blue in the face scolding and reprimanding but there'd be no remorse on her part."

"You're absolutely right."

Miss Peabody removed her hand from the jacket, pushed dishes and cutlery aside, and rested forward on the table. Others that had been sitting around her leaned away. "Whatever you might believe you have on me, you've no proof."

Decker looked at Daisy. "She's right, you know. Just because you have this paper doesn't mean a thing. There's no evidence she had anything to do with June's death. It could be a coincidence."

"But why would she pretend to be scared and now stand here in defiance? Doesn't her Dr. Jekyll-Mr. Hyde behavior tell you anything?"

"It says volumes. But we can't present her doltish behavior in a court of law. We'd be mocked and tossed out."

"But you can offer a witness on the stand." William Shanks stood in the doorway across the room from Miss Peabody.

"Shut up," The librarian snarled loudly. "You don't know a thing."

"Oh, but I do." Shanks entered with two wide strides, jaw tight and voice firm. "And I'd be happy to share everything I know after reading that folder. I had plenty of time to examine the details before your minions stole it and locked me up. I don't like being held against my will in a free country."

Decker beamed. "Well I'll be. So we have a witness and the convicted in the same place. How very convenient. Now what we need is a patrol car to take and lock you up."

"But you don't have one and you won't have a witness for very long." Peabody speed-dialed her phone then spoke to the unseen recipient. "Come over. Now. We need to get out of here."

Within minutes, the two side doors opened, one on either end of the long section. Emma Littleport, Katharyn Cutter and Barbara Bloom entered with the authority of being in charge.

"Everyone put their hands on the table, palms flat," Emma dictated, holding a canister upward. "Sodium, potassium, lithium, and other elements in the first column of the periodic table are known as alkali metals and they're extremely reactive. Believe me, you don't want to see what I can do with these chemicals."

"There's no need to harm these people." Decker

put his hands up in mock surrender. "Let them go. Then we can have a discussion by ourselves about what to do to solve this situation."

"Do you think we're fools?" Emma waddled over to Shanks. "And you. We thought we got rid of you. Thought you'd have frozen in that closet with no air or heat."

"Human nature has a strong inclination to survive. I stayed alive so that I could see you thrown in jail." William Shanks put his face close to hers. "You took a young life for no reason. I might have only recently met her, but I cared for June Fellows. Why'd you have to kill her?"

"You moron. She was no angel. She bilked us for thousands of pounds. Blackmailed each one without telling the other." Emma's face bulged with anger as she perched on tiptoes.

"What were thousands, when you were going to get millions for the confidential papers you were willing to sell? You were ready to hand over our governments top secrets to an enemy."

Emma lifted her shoulders. "The government's willing to hand over our freedom if we let them. Besides, June was a manipulator. She was no more from the south in America than I'm a pigmy from Botswana."

"Enough of this banal nattering. Let's get out of here." Miss Peabody swept up her things and stormed toward the door. "We've got to finish our transactions before we lose the deal. Otherwise none of this will be worth it."

As the four women hurried toward the exit, bright red neon lights swirled through the dining room.

Shouting, door slamming and heavy footfalls penetrated the walls as if the building was surrounded by a troop of soldiers heading into battle. "They're in there," a deep, male voice shouted.

Opening the door, the women ran headlong into a rush of police officers and were corralled back inside.

Decker smiled. "I told you what we needed were some police cars to take you out of here. They've arrived just in time."

"But, how?" Cutter screamed. "There were no phones. No way to get them here with the roads blocked. We heard it on our battery radio."

"The constabulary can be quite creative. With the help of local farmers and their plows they were able to clear the roads in no time. Besides, how were you going to escape? And how did you manage to stay warm and dry last night?"

"Don't forget, detective, we can be as resourceful

as your police force. After all, we're women. We can accomplish anything we set our minds to."

"I've no doubt you can, but you didn't answer my questions."

"We had plenty of blankets from the rooms we ransacked, plus food and supplies. We could've lasted for weeks on this group's hoard. Stealing the housemaid's keys gave us access to everything."

"And you will repay each and every person for the things you've taken."

"Except the life of June." Shanks slipped into the nearest chair and lowered his head into his hands.

"You're right. We can never replace life. But we can pursue justice to the fullest extent of the law." DS Decker laid his hand on William's shoulder.

"We'll see about that." Peabody shook off a police officer's clasp.

William raised his head. "I was certain they were going to get away with everything. June. Putting our country in harms way."

"They used this event as a cover for their schemes. What better place to try and get away with a heinous crime but at a week at a crime writing conference. I'm sure they figured if they got rid of June here, there'd be so many suspects it would take ages to solve it and they'd be long gone by then. After all, every one of you is trying to formulate the perfect murder. Your computers are filled with ways to do it. And who'd ever suspect instructors?"

"This has been a writer's winter I'll never forget," Allison said.

"Here. Here." Daisy, Val, Jen and Fiona shouted.

CHAPTER 23

The computer's fan purred as Daisy put the fob into the wall slot, and the overhead lights automatically switched on in spite of golden blocks of sunrays slicing through the bedroom.

She tossed her coat on the bed, sat on the corner and slipped off her shoes.

Ahh.

This wasn't home. Just a temporary abode. A place to start coming to terms with the maelstrom of events that turned her world upside down at Branick.

She was grateful to be alone for a few hours before packing and heading to the station. The conference was short lived but Daisy never felt more alive. Never more sure of herself. She hadn't directly solved the murder, but DS Decker had asked her advice on several occasions. She was somehow stronger and would be forever grateful. "I am woman, hear me roar." Helen Reddy's rendition slipped into her mind, and she hummed a few lines.

Daisy got up from the bed, and perched on the chair by the desk. She interlaced her fingers, stretched them several times then stroked keys on the computer. Her manuscript came into view…

A long pair of scissors plunged into the unsuspecting victim's neck. The razor-sharp edge pierced skin, tissue, and muscle. An artery burst with balloon-type pressure and spattered black-red liquid. The loser was tossed into the frozen lake, a sparkly pink cowboy hat tied to her neck. A full bottle of bubbly sat on the frozen ground beside the water...

Daisy sat back. Where *had* that bottle of bubbly come from that had been discovered at the lakeside by June's body? Why was it there?

Rap. Rap.

"Why, Fiona, come in." Daisy opened the door wide as her friend entered carrying a large Prosecco.

"I wanted you to have this. It's a gift." Fiona handed her the bottle.

"Um. How nice. Funny, this is just like the one Decker said he found near the lake."

"What do you mean?"

"Don't you remember? They discovered one the morning June was pulled from the water. Unopened."

"How strange." Fiona's eyes shifted from Daisy's eyes to the bottle in her hands. "I can't imagine where it could have come from."

"You're the only one I know that buys this brand who comes here, Fi." Daisy stepped away.

"What are you saying?"

"I'm not sure. How would one of your bottles get to the lake without you knowing?"

Fiona's tone became harsh, icy. "I don't know. I wasn't even aware it was missing until the next day. Are you trying to imply I might have something to do with June's misfortune?"

A cold shiver ran down Daisy's spine. "Of course not. I never believed it when Decker suggested you were. Remember?"

"Of course, I remember. So why would you suggest I had something to do with what happened now?"

"I'm not saying you...did...but..."

"Why Daisy, I thought we were mates. We've always had a good laugh when we've been together, haven't we?"

"Of course." Daisy circled behind Fiona and drew closer to the door in case a quick escape was needed.

"It's just that June happened to overhear me talking with Emma and Katharyn. She thought that somehow I was involved in the whole shenanigans." Fiona stepped up to her within an arm's length and reached around to push the door closed.

"And…were…you?" Daisy stepped into the gap before it slammed shut.

"I asked June to meet me at the lake after the dance. I still had the bottle with me." Fiona shrugged. "That's all."

"Why didn't you tell Decker?"

"He already thought I was guilty. If I told him I'd seen her before she died, he'd have handcuffed me straight away."

"But what *did* happen? How'd she end up wearing your hat? How'd you forget to bring your bottle with you?"

"You are so gullible."

Daisy straightened her spine. "I've heard that before, too many times, and I don't believe it anymore. In fact, I'm quite sure there's more to what's going on than you're telling me."

"They said no one would get hurt."

"Who said?"

"Emma and Katharyn, of course. Who else? They said that if I could get her away from the others that they only wanted to talk to her. They offered to pay me a huge sum to convince her to come to the lake and share some bubbly with me. She trusted me. Besides, I'd lost the competition and wouldn't be able to come next year. June didn't need the money." Fiona's tone was even, calculating. "I didn't do anything wrong."

"But you knew. You were an accomplice."

The sunrays had shifted and a slice of light cut across Fiona's face creating a frightening, distorted Halloween mask. "I needed the dosh."

Daisy held the door. Dare she run? She threw out her chest and exhaled. "If you'd told Decker this it wouldn't be a problem, but now you're going to need to confess and offer to stand as a witness in court with William. I'm sure they'll be lenient if you do."

"I'm not sure I can do that, Daisy."

"Why?"

"Because I've already deposited the money into my account before the power went out."

"You can return it. Tell the truth." Surely Fiona would see the light and take her advice.

"They don't need my confession. You said it already, Shanks will testify. And no one need know I was there that night."

"But I know."

"Yes, you might be gullible but you are also

quite clever. No one else remembered the bottle. And even if they did, they wouldn't trace it back to me."

"Please, Fi. Tell the police."

"Tell us what?" Decker came around the corner and blocked Fiona and Daisy's only means of exiting.

"Please don't say anything," Fiona mouthed the words.

""I believe my friend has something to say." Daisy directed Fiona. "And *you will* say it."

"It's been a pleasure meeting you, Daisy." DS Decker reached out his hand to shake hers.

"Thank you. You've no idea how much I appreciate what you've done for me."

"Will you ever return to Branick?" His Cadbury Button's twinkled.

"Absolutely. I'll be here in the spring when new writers will arrive to learn the craft. I wouldn't miss it for the world."

"Maybe next time you would grace me with your company for dinner?" Decker opened the cab door and Daisy slid in.

"I'd like that very much." She grinned like a

schoolgirl and waved goodbye as the taxi pulled away.

Pleasant and uneventful, the train ride gave her ample time to unwind. Undulating hills covered with snowcaps resembled Christmas cakes and Daisy opened her computer. After all, she had a New York Times Bestseller to finish and quite the story to tell.

DAISY ARRIVED at her Victorian home and waited a few seconds on the cold pavement before taking the three steps up to the entrance. Home sweet home. She loved this place.

Rosemary waved from the window and opened the front door. "Welcome home. I've some wonderful news for you."

"You do?" Daisy picked up her bags and headed inside.

"Do you want to know before or after a cuppa? I've clicked on the kettle and there are scones staying warm in the oven."

She dropped her bags on the floor. "Where's Pillow?"

"That's the news." Rosemary's facial skin couldn't stretch further with her smile.

"What is it?" Daisy's heart raced. If anything had happened to Pillow while she was gone, she'd never forgive herself.

"Go into the living room and look behind the sofa."

Daisy rushed in, heard a small mew and looked back at Rosemary. She nodded at Daisy.

Hidden behind the sofa was one of Daisy's sweaters torn to shreds. Within the threads were three tiny bodies feeding from Pillow's tummy. "She's had kittens?"

"Pillow wasn't dragging around from being overweight. She was pregnant."

"Well, I'll be."

Pillow looked up at Daisy with the mischievous grin of a magician hiding how the trick had been done.

Daisy smiled in return. "You're a natural phenomenon beyond explanation, and I can't wait for my friends to meet you and your little family."

THE END

OTHER BOOKS BY

BEATRICE FISHBACK

Fiction:

Summer of the Missing Muse:

Daisy McFarland Cozy Mystery #2

Bethel Manor

Bethel Manor Reborn

Dying to Eat at the Pub

Loving a Selfie

Christmas at the Corp

Non-fiction:

A Journal of 31 Attitudes

Loving Your Military Man

Defending the Military Marriage

Defending the Military Family

www.beasattitudes.net

Made in the USA
Columbia, SC
12 November 2020